JACK ICEFLOE JACKSON'S

ROMANCE for MEN

PANDORA'S BOX

Illustrated by
Dave McKenna

Published by
Disobedient Dragon

ROMANCE FOR MEN: PANDORA'S BOX

Cover designed by Patrick Bradley

Title treatment and logos designed by Todd Redner

Illustrated by Dave McKenna

Published by Disobedient Dragon: http://www.deanlorey.com

Digital Design by Telemachus Press, LLC: http://www.telemachuspress.com

Visit the author website: http://www.jackiceflocjackson.com

ISBN: 978-0-9903813-0-3 (eBook)

ISBN: 978-0-9903813-1-0 (Paperback)

Version 2014.05.27

Printed in the United States of America

10 9 8 7 6 5 4 3 2 1

RAVES FOR ROMANCE FOR MEN!

DENIS LEARY (*Rescue Me*) says:

"Disgusting, profane, rabid and totally unnecessary. Which is also why I LAUGHED MY ASS OFF."

SARAH MICHELLE GELLAR (*Buffy the Vampire Slayer*) says:

"ROMANCE FOR MEN is sick, depraved, and ONE OF THE FUNNIEST THINGS I'VE EVER READ! God help me, but I'm a little IN LOVE WITH ICEFLOE!"

WILL ARNETT (*Arrested Development*) says:

"A SWEEPING EPIC that speaks for a generation! ROMANCE FOR MEN establishes JACK ICEFLOE JACKSON as the TRUE LION OF AMERICAN LITERATURE. Life's too short to haven't not not read this book! IT MADE ME PUNCH A COMPLETE STRANGER!"

ROBIN WILLIAMS (*Mrs. Doubtfire*) says:

"WILDLY FUNNY, twisted, sick, and EVERY SHORT, FAT, BALD GUY'S WET DREAM."

HOWIE MANDEL (*America's Got Talent*) says:

"This is HYSTERICAL! Finally, a love story for us guys. This is FIFTY SHADES OF FUNNY!"

BRAD GARRETT (*Everybody Loves Raymond*) says:

"HYSTERICAL! And potentially the END OF CIVILIZATION…"

DAMON WAYANS (*Major Payne*) says:

"If I was short, fat and white with a TWO-INCH PENIS, I still wouldn't be as funny as Icefloe! This book is

FART-OUT-LOUD FUNNY!"

MITCH HURWITZ (creator, *Arrested Development*) says:
"One of the most DEVASTATINGLY HEARTFELT novels I've ever read. You cannot help but FALL IN LOVE with the central character in this aspirational tale of romance and, ultimately, hope. Mr. Jackson has captured the way men talk, the way they yearn and the nuance of the way they truly *feel*. To borrow a phrase from the book itself, this humanistic and insightful author seems to have 'eaten bananas and SHIT OUT A MONKEY.' And it's a GLORIOUS sort of SHIT-COVERED MONKEY indeed!"

DAVID SPADE (*Grownups*) says:
"This book did something no book can—IT SHOCKED ME! This is a wake up call for all the guys that think they have a dirty mind. ICEFLOE SCHOOLS EVERYONE. HILARIOUS. I'm LAUGHING OUT LOUD AT TACO BELL."

ADAM REED (creator, *Archer*) says:
"SMASHING! I am IN LOVE WITH JACK ICEFLOE JACKSON... and I'm okay with that."

DON REO (producer, *Two and a Half Men*) says:
"FANTASTIC!! Romance For Men is like the perfect woman: INCREDIBLY FUNNY, extremely intelligent and ABSOLUTELY FILTHY!"

KANE HODDER (Jason Voorhees, *Friday the 13th* series) says:
"SICK, TWISTED, HILARIOUS! I never thought I could be offended, but ROMANCE FOR MEN proved me wrong. ICEFLOE AND JASON WOULD MAKE THE

ULTIMATE FUCKED-UP BUDDY TEAM: Icefloe bangs chicks with his six-incher and Jason finishes them off with his machete!"

TYLER MANE (Michael Myers, *Halloween* series) says:

"INSANELY FUNNY! When kids start wearing ICEFLOE COSTUMES NEXT HALLOWEEN, we'll know THE END OF THE WORLD HAS ARRIVED..."

TODD FARMER (writer, *Jason X*, *My Bloody Valentine 3D*, *Drive Angry*) says:

"THIS IS FUCKING HILARIOUS! Jack Icefloe Jackson dicking every hot chick on Earth and dynamiting every douchebag guy to save the world from an exploding pussy? Yes, please! THIS IS THE BEST HORROR I'VE EVER READ! And don't get me started on the T&A. After reading this, I need a Viagra just to turn my dick *off*."

To guys everywhere who've had to suffer through shitty romance novels written for broads, I give you my masterpiece:

ROMANCE FOR MEN

JACK ICEFLOE JACKSON'S

ROMANCE for

MEN

PANDORA'S BOX

<u>One</u>

"YOU MUST BE getting bored of fucking me," my wife said. "Tonight you should go out and bang someone new."

She seemed serious, but it was hard to tell with bitches.

"I'm not falling for that shit," I said. "This is a trap."

"Honest to fuck," she replied as she popped off her top and started to massage nipple cream into her D-cups. "I mean, I know I have nice tits, don't get me wrong, but we've been together so long that you know every hair and vein as well as the street layout of *Grand Theft Auto: Vice City*. Face it, you need to get your hands on a new rack."

"Fuck this."

"Don't you tell me *no* when I tell you to go fuck some strange! Let's be blunt, okay? My pussy is great, and I can do some wonderful things with it if I'm drunk enough. But you deserve some hot twenty-two-year-old who can shoot fireworks out of her ass and use her tongue to make your balls sing hallelujah. And if you can't pull a sweet bitch like that and make her bark like a dog and eat a pillow tonight, you're no man of mine."

I sighed. Same old shit …

"Fine. So I go out and snag an eighteen-year-old supermodel with low self-esteem and send her a dose of religion through my six-inch shaft—"

"It feels like ten to me."

"Whatever. My point is you're gonna wanna guilt me afterwards."

"When have I ever guilted you?"

"Never. But there's a first time for everything."

"Look," she said, and I knew she was serious because she had the same tone she always used when she begged me to flip her over and visit her chocolate starfish with my meatstick, "If I so much as give you even the slightest shred of guilt about this, as punishment I demand you go fuck my sister."

"Which one? The hot one or the super-hot one?"

"The super-hot one, obviously. The one with natural double D's and an ass that looks like a ventriloquist dummy's chin."

"You're talking about the nineteen-year-old born without a gag reflex?"

She nodded. "It's one of the world's most criminally underfunded birth defects."

I sighed. "Fine. I'll go bang some strange tonight and give her the sexy shakes. But if I come back here and you eyeroll me about it, I may not choose to plow your nineteen-year-old supermodel sister with the giant natural tits and no gag reflex. I may just decide to take your twenty-two-year-old physicist sister with full lips and legs so long they split more than atoms when you part them and give her my own big bang theory. Are we clear?"

"Not only are we clear," she replied, "if I eyeroll you, I demand you do both my sisters at the same time."

"Come on …"

"YOU WILL FUCK BOTH OF MY HOT SISTERS OR I WILL EAT A SHOTGUN! GOT IT?"

I sighed. "Fine. But remember, you asked for this shit."

"I did. Now go out and find a bitch so sweet she's as mythical as a unicorn and fuck her deep and long until I get done baking your favorite pumpkin pie."

"Put rum in it," I said as I headed out into the night.

Two

I WALKED INTO Whisky Bill's and announced: "I'm looking to bang someone."

"That just made me so wet," said the knockout at the end of the bar.

The place was lousy with models. Whisky Bill's had a strict "No Wine and No Whining" policy that was enforced by Bill himself, a beefy fuck with a nose that looked like an orangutan's sack. He kept the beer flowing, the music loud and the models happy, although they knew not to interrupt your pool shot or complain about the moose heads on the wall or out the fucking door they went.

I sat down at an empty bar stool, and the knockout came over to me like I was the Nativity and she was all three Wise Men rolled up into the body of a tall blonde bitch with killer tits and green eyes so innocent they had yet to see the sweaty underside of a pair of balls. I could tell just by looking at her that she had an asshole like King Tut's tomb. Once it was plundered, there were treasures inside.

"How overweight are you?" she asked.

I patted my belly. "Thirty, thirty-five pounds."

"That's so fucking hot."

I nodded. I knew it was.

"When did you start losing your hair?"

"Early twenties, I guess."

She shuddered in pleasure. "Holy shit. I just want to lick your bald head and keep going south."

She had an accent. French or Japanese or Guatemalan maybe. As if it mattered.

"So here's the deal," I said. "I'm gonna fuck one of these broads tonight, maybe you if you play your cards right. But I'm not in the mood to buy anyone a drink, and if you're looking for foreplay beyond my standard line, which is 'Open your pussy,' you may as well just pick that perfect ass up off the bar stool so I can snag the next hot bitch who knows what the hell time it is."

"Sold."

I took her to my truck and banged her to within an inch of her life.

"I got enough gas in the tank to finish you off," I said, after a solid minute of slapping steaks.

She shook her head. "I don't want you to make me feel good. I only want to make *you* feel good. I want you to cum like you've never cum before!"

"Don't flatter yourself. I've been in the cumming business since before you were born, and I'm more likely to spot a yeti than blow my load in some exotic new way. You sure you don't want me to give you a quick screaming O? I'll make you cum so hard you'll break a hip."

"Sounds great, but I only want to please you."

"Whatever."

Right after I shot my milkshake on her face, I was startled by a knock on the door. I rolled down the window. It was Bill.

"Got some bad news for you," he said.

"Yeah?"

"Just got a call. Your wife's dead."

Three

IT WAS SUICIDE. Pills. There was no clean up, and I appreciated Tina for that. She left a note:

> *Dear Jack Icefloe Jackson,*
>
> *I know you don't like to read, so I'll keep this short: You deserve better. The next time you're hot mopping the forehead of some beautiful Thai princess, just know that there's an angel up in heaven whispering in your ear, "Shoot that load, big daddy! Shoot that load!"*
>
> *Love you forever,*
> *Tina*

The note was tucked underneath a fresh pumpkin pie, still warm. I ate a slice. It had rum in it, just the way I liked.

She was a good one, my Tina.

The funeral was the next day, and I was concerned it wouldn't be a lot of fun. Mothers of dead wives can be tricky, and this particular mother was a firecracker in a fat suit. Plus, she was crafty. The kind of bitch who could eat bananas and shit out a monkey.

"What's up, Flo?" I said.

"I miss my daughter."

Jesus Christ. I expected a little drama but give me a fucking break. I nodded, trying to control my anger. "Yeah, it sucks."

"Oh, how she loved you, Jack. She worshipped you. To her, you were a golden god." Then the waterworks started. Her eyes sprayed a stream of tears like a bulldog pissing on a tree.

"Ah, don't do that," I said. "No, seriously, don't do that. I don't like it."

She stopped crying.

From behind me I heard a new voice, one with a little cock in it. "Jack." I turned to see Bob, my dead wife's father. His eyes were puffy from crying. He held a six-pack. "Want a Coors? They're chilled. We'll drink to my girl."

"What the hell, why not?"

We cracked open a couple cold ones and drank to dead Tina. Kind of sentimental, I know, but that didn't make me a gayboy. In case you're wondering, here's the rules on being a gayboy:

RULES FOR BEING A GAYBOY

If you don't go in past the tip—*not a gayboy.*

If you get no pleasure from fucking a dude and your heart is filled with hate while you do it—*not a gayboy.*

If you've drunk enough whisky to legally blow a .28 or higher—*not a gayboy.*

BUT:

If you let a dude fuck you—*gayboy.*

If you enjoy fucking a dude—*gayboy.*

BY THE WAY:

There is nothing wrong with being a gayboy. God
made different people in the world, the same way
he made different color M&M's. God made red
M&M's and yellow M&M's and gayboy M&M's.
There is nothing wrong with this.

DON'T JUDGE.

So Bob and I polished off a couple cans of suds. "What do you
think you'll do now?" he asked, wiping foam from his mustache.

"Fuck someone new, I guess."

He nodded. "Makes sense. Flo said Tina killed herself
because she thought you deserved better. Well, you do. You're a
helluva man, Jack Icefloe Jackson. You deserve the world and all
the pussy in it. And I know you made my daughter real happy
before she swallowed those hundred Oxycontin. She liked to tell
me how great you were at banging her in the anus."

I shrugged. Anal banging is one of my many specialties.

"I can't figure out how the Lord made such a perfect guy,"
Bob said, then glanced down at the lump in my stained jeans.
"It's like you got a couple extra nuts in your sack. Like you got
four jism factories in your soft pouch where the rest of us gotta
make due with two."

"I just got the regular amount of nuts."

"It don't seem that way. What's it like to be you?"

"Fucking great."

"I bet."

He cracked open the last couple beers and handed me one
when someone said: "Jack Icefloe Jackson, I want you to fuck the

shit out of me right on my dead sister's coffin!"

I looked over. It was Tina's smoking hot nineteen-year-old supermodel sister with the natural double D's and no gag reflex. She walked over to the edge of the gravesite, causing some dirt to crumble and fall onto the coffin below. "Take me," she continued, before jumping into the hole and landing on the coffin with a thud. "Fuck me now, on my sister's corpse! Fuck me, to honor *her*!"

Four

"WHAT'S UP, CANDY?" I said as she looked up at me, tits spilling from her tank top like oil from the Exxon Valdez.

"Your cock, I hope."

"You talk that way in front of your father?"

Bob just shrugged. "It's okay. I know what close proximity to you can do to a person. My daughter's only human."

"But my pussy is divine," Candy said. "Want to taste it?" She gave me a flash of her beaver, and I noticed she'd pierced her spicy-lips with silver jewelry that had the letters J.I.J. inscribed on it. Jack Icefloe Jackson.

I shook my head. "Come on up out of there. You're embarrassing yourself."

"Only after you come down here and fuck me! I've wanted you for so long. Even Tina knew it was wrong to keep you all to herself. She promised you'd give me a solid dicking for my twentieth birthday."

"She was always generous that way."

Candy nodded. "If you don't come down here and use me

like a toilet bowl handle, I'm going to make a scene."

I wondered what kind of scene she could be referring to, considering she was already laying spread eagle on the coffin of her dead sister, legs split like fire logs. Some of the other mourners were beginning to take notice. It was unseemly.

"No," I said. "Go find someone else to fuck you."

"There is no one else, only you! My pussy is untouched by man. It's been on layaway until I could have you. Now I want you to unwrap it and explore its mysteries, mapping it like Lewis and Clark mapped the New World ..."

"Just the Northwest," I mumbled, but she was stroking her pussy with an oversized black dildo, so geographical niceties were probably beyond her. I sighed. "You sure are one crazy bitch."

She nodded, eyes as wild as a lab rat's. "Take me," she moaned.

The upside with crazy bitches was that they usually made for good fucking.

I once spent three white-knuckle days banging a smoking hot suicide bomber named Ishfaq who liked to rock cock while wearing her explosive vest. The sight of her giant juggs bouncing on either side of a stick of dynamite made for mind blowing steak slapping, the kind that makes you reach for the Neosporin right after you cum to begin triage. Unfortunately, it ended up being short-lived, just like Ishfaq.

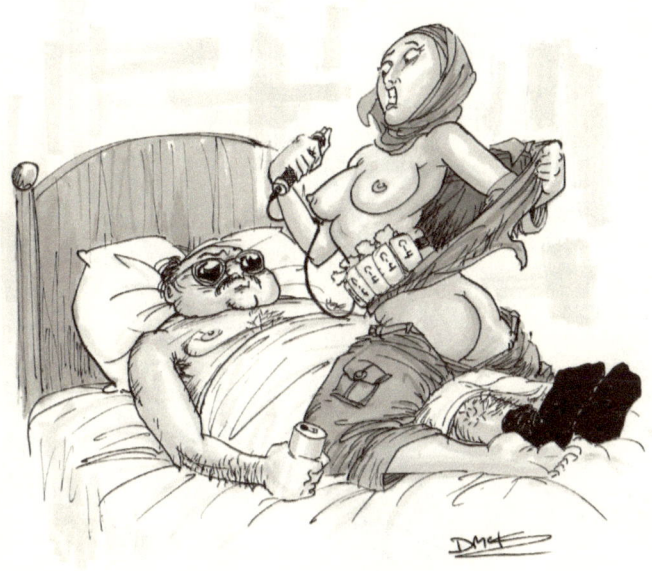

After one particularly hot porkathon, she headed to the bathroom to take off the vest and towel off. Unfortunately, a kid in the apartment next door was playing *Dance Dance Revolution* at exactly the same radio frequency as the detonator. Ishfaq blew a hole in the side of the building you could send a SWAT team through, which is exactly what came storming in twenty minutes later. By then, of course, I was across town, banging a Kenyan ultramarathon runner whose name you could only pronounce with clicks.

"Fuck me now!" Candy screamed, leaping to her feet on the coffin. "Do me like you did my sister!"

"He's mine, you loony bitch!" another voice shouted and, moments later, my dead wife's *other* sister, the twenty-two-year-old with the PhD in physics and an ass so hot you could cook a trout on it, leapt down onto the coffin and bit Candy on the shoulder like a jungle cat in heat.

Five

LIKE ALL MEN, I love a good catfight. Few things make your cock heavier than hot women acting like beasts just so their pussies can get invaded by your junk.

"Oww!" Candy screamed, grabbing her bleeding shoulder. "Fuck you, Marcy!" Then Candy leaned back and kicked Marcy in the uterus.

"You whore!" Marcy said. "Anywhere but my uterus! Don't you know you don't kick a woman in her uterus?" And then the fists started flying. Hair got pulled and clothes got ripped and within seconds four perfect tits hit the air, bouncing out of torn blouses. I let the fight go on for a while until the whole thing started seeming inappropriate.

"Bitches?" I said. "Excuse me, crazy bitches?"

Candy was trying to suffocate Marcy with her hot box, and they were both in such a frenzy that they couldn't hear me.

"*Bitches, enough!*" I yelled.

That got through. They both looked up at me, mostly naked now and covered in blood and grave dirt, which I'll admit only made them look hotter.

"Yes, Jack Icefloe Jackson?" Candy asked.

"I don't know who the hell raised you—"

"I did," Candy's mom, Flo, said raising her hand.

"Right. Well, I bet you didn't teach them to catfight on their sister's grave just to get speared with some of the best cock the Lord ever miracled."

"It never came up," Flo said. "Although it does seem wrong."

"So you're not going to fuck us?" Marcy asked, wiping blood from her nose with the same hand she used to calculate moonshots for NASA.

I shook my head. "Don't you have any morality? Don't you have any common fucking *decency*? No, I am not going to fuck you on your sister's grave." The bitches looked crestfallen. "I will, however, let you blow me and lick my taint."

That perked them up. Moments later, I was on my back on the coffin, and Candy was working my meatpole with lips so soft and strong they could suck a cat off a chimney while Marcy cleaned my taint with a tongue as agile as a flutist from the Royal Philharmonic. To my surprise, I was finding it a little hard to cum with Tina's family and friends looking down at me from around the open grave. And then I heard it. Like an angel whispering in my ear, my beautiful Tina spoke to me from the afterlife: "*Shoot that load, big daddy! Shoot that load!*"

I did, then looked up to heaven and winked. *Thanks, angel.* A few minutes later, I was standing at the foot of Tina's grave, delivering her eulogy.

"My Tina thought she didn't deserve me, and she didn't. Hell, what woman does?" The women standing around the gravesite all nodded in understanding. "I gotta say though, she came pretty close. Most people just thought of her as Jack Icefloe Jackson's bitch, but she had some accomplishments of her own. I'm thinking of her Nobel Peace Prize for helping to eradicate malaria. Winning Miss Universe a couple years back was also nothing to sneeze at. And we shouldn't forget the Pope naming her a living saint, which can't be all that common. So there's that stuff. But let's talk about me. Will I miss her? Of course I wi—"

I would have finished the sentence, except my eye was caught by a tour bus rolling to a stop with the words "Porn Star Oral/Anal Tour!" written on the side. The doors opened, and a big-titted beast in high heels stepped out.

"Jack Icefloe Jackson!" she shouted.

"Yeah?"

"We need you to come here and fuck us."

The windows opened, and a couple dozen of the most famous bitches in porn stuck their heads out and waved to me.

"*All of us!*"

Six

THERE WAS MORE silicone in that bus than a newly weatherproofed house. If I had a dollar for every fake tit and plumped lip roaming around in there, I would have had enough to go dynamite fishing for walleye pike, something you should try if you haven't. There's nothing more satisfying than rupturing the swim bladder of unsuspecting marine creatures with a bomb made of ammonium nitrate and kerosene, then seeing the bloated little fuckers float to the surface like used condoms in a cathouse toilet.

I stepped onto the bus after saying goodbye to the mourners. They all understood, especially Tina's dad, Bob.

"Hey, I'd fuck 'em if they'd have me," he said. "But I ain't Jack Icefloe Jackson."

"Nope," I replied. "Hardly anyone is."

The big-titted beast on the bus seemed happy to see me, and she showed her pleasure by going down on another porn star who I vaguely recognized as a star of over two hundred of the finest entertainments ever stuck to tape. She'd won the *Adult Video News* award for best novelty scene three years running by stuffing two anaconda-sized cocks into her asshole while wearing a Princess Leia costume.

I have a theory on big cocks, by the way: When anything larger than a dirty water hot dog gets hard, it drains too much blood from your skull, depriving you of your biggest and most necessary organ. Your brain. And I don't say this in a "women want a smart guy" sort of way, because they don't, although the stupider ones think they do. I say this because a real man has to have all his faculties about him at all times because bitches are tricky.

Everything about them is a lie.

They cover their faces with makeup to hide the fact that they all really look like Joan River's loudmouthed daughter's asshole. They wear bras to make their small tits bigger and girdles to make their big stomachs smaller and contact lenses to make their ugly brown eyes blue. They color their hair to get rid of the gray and inject themselves with poison to erase wrinkles and fool you into thinking they're twenty years younger than they really are. Don't believe me? Strip all that shit off a supermodel, and you'll end up fucking a warthog with tits.

"So what do you want from me?" I asked the big-titted beast as she lapped away at a porn star like a gazelle at a watering hole.

"We don't want anything *from* you, we want to *give* you something …"

All the bitches dropped to their knees and opened their mouths. They looked like baby birds sitting in a nest, awaiting cock.

"You all want to suck me off?"

"Please! Please! Please!" they begged.

"Fine. Let's say I let you. What's in it for me?"

All eyes turned to a small room in the back of the bus. I could see a length of ivory leg and a flash of blonde hair.

"Who's that?" I asked.

The big-titted beast smiled. "That's the *prize*. If you can survive us, you get a shot at fucking Siren."

Siren. I'd heard of her. She was as beautiful as she was frigid. No one had ever thawed her perfect pussy enough to give her the sexy shakes. It was said there was a prize for any man who succeeded. A BIG prize.

"I'll take a crack at her."

"You have to get past us first," the big-titted beast replied. "But be warned: Most men slip into a coma before even getting halfway."

"I'm not most men. Prepare, bitches. You have entered the fuckatorium of Jack Icefloe Jackson, and you will leave here changed."

I took out my cock and waded in.

Seven

IT WAS A tidal wave of pussy, but I schooled every open mouth and gaping hole with four inches of prime, patriotic American flagpole. I say four inches because no whore alive could take the full six. The bitches thought every jism jolt was going to be my last, but they didn't know that my record was ninety-three separate sperm blasts in a row.

That particular accomplishment had occurred after-hours at a renaissance festival in Youngstown, Ohio. Those "Medieval Faires" are basically delivery systems for cleavage, designed to satisfy the desires of middle-aged dads who try to pawn the whole titfest off as a learning experience for their retardo spawn.

"Do you ever stop?" a porn star known as Anal something-or-other gasped, wiping my spunk from her left eye as I came for the seventh time.

I shrugged. "If my cock were a car, it would be a Prius because I get a shitload of mileage out of it. By the way, bitches, I'm not recommending you buy a douchemobile like that. Far as I'm concerned, you either get a Ford F-150 or you can go fuck yourself with an Arab's dick."

"Gotcha," she said as I continued cocking my way to the very back of the bus. When I got there, I turned around to survey the damage. Porn stars were scattered around like crumbs on a fat kid's belly. Their faces looked like glazed donuts.

"Anyone else?" I asked. "Or should I just head into the back room and slip Siren the sweetest shaft she's ever seen?"

"Go fuck her," the big-titted beast said. "God knows you've earned it."

"Yes, he has!" the other porn stars gasped. "He sure has!"

I headed into the back room to find as perfect a bitch as I'd ever seen in my entire life. Her hair was the kind of blonde that could only come out of a bottle if it was filled with God's spunk. Her blue eyes were the color of a dead girl's lips, and her skin was as tight as a baby's asshole.

"Hey, Siren," I said. "Word is you've never cum."

She shook her head slowly. "Never."

"Then you mind if I take a crack at your crack?"

"Feel free," she replied with a voice that sounded like what I imagined the Virgin Mary would sound like if she was being double teamed by Sudanese pirates in the hold of a Japanese cargo ship.

I smiled. "Then open your pussy and let the banging begin."

She did, and I went to work. After two solid minutes of straight cocking, she had barely even moaned, which was troubling. Usually at that point, bitches were unconscious and I was toweling off.

"You're a tough one," I said

She nodded. "You better believe it. And you're not gonna make me cum."

"Sweetheart, I'm gonna break you like the Enigma code."

I flipped her over and started working her from behind, resting my fat belly on her perfect ass. After a couple more minutes, a moan escaped her lips. Unfortunately, sweat had beaded across my bald head. I couldn't remember the last time I'd pumped hard enough to make that happen.

"Getting tired?" she asked.

"Just getting started. Won't be much longer. Know why? Because I got a secret. Wanna hear it?"

"Sure."

"I only been fucking you with four inches. See how you like five." I slipped her the fifth inch, and the reaction was immediate. She bucked like a calf on branding day.

"Oh, my God!" she gasped. "Oh, my fucking God!"

"That's right, baby. The Lord is speaking to you through my shaft. Can you even imagine if I gave you all six? You'd shit yourself and go blind."

"Cock me, Icefloe! Fuck me with your freaky five!"

I did, and when she finally came, she orgasmed so hard she kicked a hole through the side of the bus and ripped the closet door off its hinges. I had broken the unbreakable. I pulled out of her, drenched in sweat, as she spasmed a few times and then went deathly still, eyes closed.

"Hey, Siren," I said. "You didn't just fucking die on me, did you?"

No reply. The other bitches on the bus came into the room, frightened.

"Is she …?" the Anal something-or-other one asked.

I nodded. "Looks like it. I think I cocked her to death. I

probably shouldn't have given her the extra inch. No woman can take all that."

Suddenly, Siren's eyes snapped open, and I was shocked to see that they were now tiny computer screens. She began to speak, and when she did, it was with someone else's voice: "Congratulations, Jack Icefloe Jackson. You have done what no other man on Earth could do. You have successfully given the XXX-69 Unit its first orgasm."

Jesus Christ, I realized. *She's a Fuck-Bot ...*

Eight

"WHAT THE HELL is this all about?" I asked. "Who are you?"

The woman speaking through the Fuck-Bot continued. "We have much to discuss, but it's highly classified. You will learn all you need to know quite soon. For the moment, I can only tell you that your government—and the world—needs you. There is a looming global threat that only someone with your unique skills can neutralize."

"Does it require superior cocking ability?"

The Fuck-Bot nodded, making her perfectly sculpted tits bounce. "I wouldn't have put it exactly that way, but yes. We dispatched this bus to scour the country, looking for the greatest lover in the United States. Very few men had the nerve to even attempt to service a bus filled with porn stars. Of those who tried, only a dozen successfully made their way to the back of the bus, where this XXX-69 Unit is located."

"You say XXX-69 Unit, I say Fuck-Bot."

The Fuck-Bot shrugged. "Whatever you want to call it, it is the government's greatest technological achievement. Of the twelve men who attempted to bring the 'Fuck-Bot' as you call it to orgasm, you are the only one to succeed. In all fairness, it's a nearly impossible task. On the PFO scale—that is, Potential For Orgasm—with ten being the hardest to please and one being a female who is brought to climax by too-tight jeans, most women fall in the three to six range."

"What's the Fuck-Bot set at?"

"A hundred and ninety-two. You have a greater chance of getting hit by a meteor than bringing the XXX-69 Unit to orgasm, and yet you *did*. You are one-of-a-kind, Jack Icefloe Jackson, and your government needs you."

"So what do you want me to do?"

"A helicopter should be landing shortly."

I looked out the window and saw a Lockheed Martin VH-71 Kestrel with a ground speed of 155 miles per hour settling onto the pavement. There were only a handful of these puppies in the world and each one cost a cool half-billion. They were reserved for the president.

"It's here," I said.

"Good. Get on it. It will bring you to me and I will brief you further."

"Alright. But before I do ..."

"Yes?"

"I want you to reset the Fuck-Bot with a PFO of two hundred and fifty."

The Fuck-Bot seemed shocked. "Why on Earth would you want me to do that?"

"Because I want to fuck it again and, this time, I want a *challenge*."

"Mr. Jackson, please, no human on Earth can bring the

XXX-69 to climax with a PFO of two fifty. Besides, we hardly have the time for you to—"

I stood to leave. "See you around, sweetheart. I only hope someone over there has the kind of magic cock you're looking for because my interest in this whole deal is going as limp as my pecker."

"Alright, alright! I'll reset it. But, please, hurry. And be careful! The fate of the world rests on your penis. We don't dare damage it."

I laughed. "Babe, this cock is like Pearl Harbor. Not even a thousand Japs with bombs could prevent it from becoming a tourist destination. Now reset the Fuck-Bot. I want to get to work."

Eight minutes later I brought the Fuck-Bot to such a screaming orgasm that its eyes popped out and its left tit shot across the room. The head started to smoke, and pretty soon the whole damn thing was engulfed in flames.

"You destroyed the XXX-69!" the woman speaking through the Fuck-Bot yelled, although her voice was distorted because the robot's throat was melting.

"Sorry. I know it was a pricey gizmo, but sometimes that happens when Jack Icefloe Jackson unleashes the fifth inch."

"My God, you didn't even use all six?!"

I shook my head. "No, ma'am. I've never used the sixth inch, and I never will. It might cause a rip in the fabric of time."

"Get on that chopper!" the woman screamed right before the entire Fuck-Bot exploded in a shower of fake ass and pussy. I wiped a piece off my face, then said my goodbyes to the porn stars and hopped onto the waiting VH-71 Kestrel.

"Where we headed?" I asked the pilot.

"The White House," he replied as we lifted off.

Nine

"MY NAME IS Ms. Cherry," said the woman who had been speaking to me earlier through the Fuck-Bot. She was the kind of bitch that conceals a body made for sex under a stuffy business suit, the same way drug traffickers hide balloons of heroin in their rectum to avoid being sent to Turkish prison camps to be gang raped by Armenians. "So, what do you think of the White House?"

I shrugged. "It's alright."

"Just alright? Most people are impressed by the beauty of it. The history."

"Nah."

"Oh. Well, okay. Please, come in." She ushered me into her office and shut the door behind me. I noticed she was a redhead, which meant her pussy tasted like tinfoil. She took a seat behind her desk, and I sat down on the chair in front of it.

"So what kind of bullshit have you gotten this country into that you need me to fix?" I asked.

"You'll be briefed in full shortly. Until then, I have a few questions for you. Nothing serious. Strictly informational."

"Shoot."

She took out a pad of paper and a red, white and blue pen that said "White House" on it. "Okay, to begin, where do you currently live?"

"Right here."

She started to write that down, then stopped. "I'm sorry, what?"

"Look, sweetheart, home is where my dick is, so right now I live here in the White House with you."

"I'm going to put down *homeless*."

I shrugged. "Whatever twists your tits."

She wrote something on her pad and continued. "Alright, do you have any hobbies?"

I nodded. "Two. Dynamite hunting and fucking Chinese bitches."

"Interesting. Why specifically Chinese women?"

"I thought that was obvious. Because they so horny."

She stared at me. Jesus, she was as dumb as a moon rock. Finally, she scratched something down on her pad and continued. "Alright, because of the nature of the challenge ahead, I'm interested in knowing a little bit about how you connect emotionally to women."

"What do you mean?"

"Well, for instance, what do you talk about when you have a conversation with a woman?"

"I'm not following."

"Okay. You know how sometimes you'll talk to women?"

"You mean about fucking?"

"No, just regular conversation."

"With who?"

"With a woman."

"Wait—what?"

I was beginning to feel light headed. I had no idea what she was getting at. It was as if the red-headed bitch was speaking Korean.

"I just don't know what you mean," I said finally.

She looked at me over her glasses. "Let me try it this way: I just want to know what you say to women when you talk to them about something *other* than sex."

"Are you having a stroke or—"

"I'm trying to understand how you connect with women on an emotional level."

"Emotional meaning … fucking?"

"No, not sexually. *Emotionally.*"

"I see." I swallowed. "Actually, I don't see. Can you say the same thing but with different words?"

I could tell from the way she was biting her upper lip hard enough to draw blood that she was getting frustrated, but it was like trying to communicate with a yak. "Okay, forget all this talk about conversation," she continued. "Let's talk about action. You know how you'll sometimes do things with women just for fun?"

"No."

"No? You've never done something with a woman just to have a good time?"

"Wait, yes. You mean fucking?"

"No, *not* fucking." She took a deep breath. "I mean, not sexual intercourse. I'm asking what kinds of things you do with women that have nothing to do with sex."

I suddenly realized it was a trick question that didn't have a real answer, like "When did you stop ass-plowing your goat?" I chuckled. "Heh, I see what you're doing. You almost got me there."

"What do you mean I almost *got* you? I'm not trying to get you, I'm just asking a question."

"So you're serious?"

"Yes, I'm fucking serious!"

She took another one of those deep breaths. "Okay, let me try again. In what way, *other than through sex*, do you spend time with women?"

"You mean when I'm not fucking them?"

"Correct."

"And by fucking, do you include anal in that definition?"

"Yes, anal sex is still sex."

"What about finger banging?"

"I don't want to hear about finger banging, either. I'm talking about things that have nothing at all to do with sex."

"Gotcha. How about when I let them suck my balls?"

She pushed back angrily from her desk when the intercom

buzzed. "What?" she snapped.

"The President is ready for Mr. Icefloe Jackson," a voice on the other end said.

"Thank God." She turned to me. "Alright. I'm going to escort you to him. Have you ever met the President before?"

I shook my head. "Nope."

"Well, he wants to brief you on this mission personally. Don't be nervous, you'll do just fine."

"Hell, why would I be nervous? I didn't even vote for him. C'mon, let's go see the fucker."

Ten minutes later, I was standing in front of President Barack Hussein Obama.

Ten

"I APPRECIATE YOU coming to see me on such short notice," Obama said as we stood in the oval office. He was taller in person than he seemed on TV. I sensed he was packing something serious between his legs, at least an eight incher, although I had concerns about its girth.

"No problem," I said. "You ever think about the amount of spunk that's been spilled here?"

That seemed to give Obama pause. "What do you mean?"

"Just that presidents like to bang. Between Monica Lewinsky and Marilyn Monroe, I'm guessing that one of those blue lights from CSI would make this place look like the inside of the Millenium Falcon. Speaking of which, do you guys have aliens over there in Area 51?"

"I can't really comment on that."

"Okay. But are they hot? I mean, would you fuck them?"

"No."

"So you admit they exist. That's okay, I won't tell anyone. Me? I'd probably bang one just for the hell of it. Do they have multiple alien pussies, or just the one?"

"Mr. Jackson, please have a seat," Obama said and gestured to the couch. We both sat down. "I appreciate you coming to talk to me about a matter of such grave importance."

I shrugged. "Sure. But we should get something straight right from the top. I didn't vote for you, and I question the thickness of your dick."

"That's fine. I don't need you to vote for me, Mr. Jackson, and my penis is perfectly—"

"Garden hose thick?" I interrupted.

There was a long pause. "Baby leg."

"Damn. Nice."

"But, as I said," Obama continued, "I don't need you to vote for me. Frankly, I need you to fuck for me."

"I'm listening."

He leaned forward. "Have you ever heard of Pandora?"

"The mythical bitch with the killer box?"

The President nodded. "Yes. But this is a different Pandora, and her box isn't an actual object."

"You're talking about her box as in *her pussy*?"

He nodded. "Yes. She is, without question, the most beautiful woman alive. Perhaps the most beautiful woman that has ever existed."

"You just made my cock twitch like a Mexican jumping bean. Go on."

"Unfortunately, Pandora is as deadly as she is beautiful. At birth, she was afflicted with a curse to punish her for her spectacular body. If she doesn't achieve orgasm by the time she turns twenty-one, her vagina will explode and become a black hole that will destroy all human life and plunge our world into an abyss of horror."

I whistled. "That's some pussy."

"Indeed. Pandora is currently twenty years old. Her birthday is in one week. You, Mr. Jackson, need to find her, fuck her and bring her to climax or everything and everyone we know will perish."

"Well, you came to the right guy. Good thing I cock well under pressure." I stood up. "So, she around? I'll go give her a quick bang in the Lincoln Bedroom while you polish up a medal for me."

"I'm afraid it's not that simple."

It never fucking is, is it? I sat back down. "Alright, so what's the catch?"

"First, you're going to need to meet with a … lady … to find out the current location of Pandora and get fully briefed on the most up-to-date techniques for dealing with her."

"I don't like the way you paused before you said *lady*. We must be talking some serious skank here, the kind that has a pussy that smells like blue cheese. Am I right?"

"Well, I'll agree that the lady is something less than savory," Obama conceded. "She is known as the Bitch Witch."

"Because?"

"Because she's a witch. And sort of bitchy. But she knows a lot about curses, and she will provide you with invaluable assistance."

"Fine. Where is she?"

"New York. We'll send you there on a military jet. You'll leave in two hours, after we outfit you with a variety of monitors and sensors so we can keep track of your progress."

I shook my head. "Negatory. I don't work for you, and I sure as hell am not gonna let you peep at my pecker while I'm mining for clit."

Obama chuckled. "I understand, but we're talking about a

potentially world-ending event here. A game changer for the entire planet. It's critical that we keep tabs on your progress."

"Nope. If you want me to save your ass from this shitstorm, I do it on my own."

"I'm afraid I have to insist."

"I said no."

I thought I'd made myself perfectly clear, but the cocksucker didn't seem to understand that "No Means No" is one of the fundamental rules of manly conversation. Just in case you don't know them, I'll go over them real quick:

RULES OF MANLY CONVERSATION

1) No means no. No explanation necessary. No questions asked.

2) You do not give reasons, you give answers. (*Acceptable*: "I can't make it Monday night." *Unacceptable*: "Monday night is hard for me because I forgot that Monday night is date night with my wife, and I also need to help my retardo kids with their homework because I am a giant, hairy pussy.")

3) You never "share" or talk about "feelings" or act like you "give a shit" about "anything." (*Only exception*: Another guy's dad just died, in which case you can say "that sucks" but if you follow that up with crying, you deserve to be mouth-cocked with donkey dick.)

4) A man's word is his bond, unless you're *James* Bond, and then you sometimes have to lie so you can save the world from Goldfinger.

In any event, this Obama didn't seem to understand that "No

Means No." He smiled that same smile that conned millions of grown up retardos to vote for him. "I appreciate your confidence in your own abilities," he said, "but you cannot go rogue on this. You must allow us to keep a close watch on your progress."

"You saying you don't trust me?"

"I'm saying I don't trust *anyone* with something this important."

I jumped to my feet. "Say you don't trust me again! Go on, say it again, and I will come over there and fuck you in your asshole—which doesn't make me a gayboy, because I'll do it with hate in my heart."

Obama stumbled back, and I could tell by the way the Secret Service agents were leveling their weapons at my head and shouting, "He's threatening to fuck the President in the ass!" that they were getting a little anxious.

Eleven

OBAMA RAISED HIS hands. "Let's just calm down, okay? Let's lower the temperature a bit."

"Fine by me," I replied, sitting back down. The Secret Service agents seemed to relax after the threat of ass banging the President had lessened. "I'm just saying, I do this my way or I don't do it at all. Which means I go it alone."

"I understand," Obama said. "But this could involve some travel. How do you plan to get around?"

"With the million dollars cash you're about to give me. You have that much on you?"

"No, but we can print some."

"Do it."

Obama nodded to an aide, who rushed out of the room. "Okay, we'll get you your money," he said, turning back. "But keep in mind that with anything this important, there's always the potential for danger."

"I'll be fine. There's nothing in this world I haven't killed."

"You're a hunter?"

I nodded. "Yup. Ever since I was a kid. I've handled just about every weapon known to man, although now I mostly favor dynamite. Dynamite hunting is a little known but enormously satisfying specialty."

Obama was beginning to get little creases in his brow, what my Grandma used to call "worry lines" before she died, which is when she stopped talking.

"Hmmm," he said. "Dynamite hunting. I've never heard of it. I've heard of dynamite *fishing*."

"Love that. It's one of my two favorite hobbies, along with fucking Chinese bitches."

"Because they so horny?" Obama asked.

I nodded. "Exactly." Score one for the Big Man. "But dynamite hunting can be even more fun than dynamite fishing. There are few pleasures in this world greater than seeing the look of surprise on a deer's face as it laps water from a spring-fed lake after you lob a stick of TNT at it and blow its hindquarters off."

A couple more creases formed on Obama's brow. "That hardly seems sporting."

"Hell, it's just the opposite. See, dynamite is the most dangerous weapon a hunter can use. You have to light the fuse and wait to throw it until the very last second, or you'll frighten your prey before it explodes. The timing is very tricky and mistakes can be costly. Just ask my hunting buddies One-Armed Pete and No-Jaw Johnson or even Rod-the-Quad, although anyone who takes a cell phone call while holding a lit stick of dynamite deserves what he gets."

Obama shook his head in something like wonder. "I can't believe I've never heard of this before."

"Pardon me, Mr. President, but what you don't know could fill the long ball sacks of all the eighty-year-old men in the world."

The President laughed. "Maybe you're right. Do you mind if I ask what you do with your prey once you've killed it?"

"Eat it, the way God intended. Hell, I make a dynamite black bear chili."

"Dynamite as in method of execution or dynamite as in taste?"

"You're goddamn right," I said, and then I told him how I make it. If you want to make it yourself, here's the recipe:

ICEFLOE'S DYNAMITE BLACK BEAR CHILI

1) Dynamite a black bear and cut off its ass.

2) Dice and brown the ass.

3) Add 1 cup onion and 2 cloves garlic, finely chopped.

4) Then add 2 (16-ounce) cans kidney beans, drained and rinsed, along with 2 teaspoons chili powder and 1/2 teaspoon ground cumin.

5) Bring to a boil. Reduce heat to low; cover. Cook, stirring frequently, for 20 to 25 minutes.

6) Garnish as desired before serving. I use Italian parsley.

Obama thanked me for the recipe, although I doubted he'd ever use it. "So what else can I do for you before you head out to save us all?" he asked.

"Nothing," I said. "Except I'm gonna need a license to kill."

"A what?"

"A license to kill. Like James Bond has. Hell, you yourself said this might be dangerous."

"Yes, but we don't just hand out licenses to kill. I mean, if we did, everyone would want one."

I shrugged. "Suit yourself. I just hope *you* can fuck this chick into a bout of the sexy shakes, because I'm done." I stood to go.

"Alright, fine," Obama said, defeated. "You can have your license to kill."

"Thought you'd see it my way. Now where do I find this Bitch Witch?"

He leaned toward me. "Bloomingdale's in Manhattan. She works in women's shoes."

Twelve

I DECIDED TO fly Cuntinental to New York. You may notice that that's not the actual name of the airline. That's because I have a policy of not calling airlines by their real names because I hate all of them because they all suck dick. Except for Virgin for obvious reasons.

My rocky relationship with airlines began in the mid-nineties when I was flying to the convention center in Nome, Alaska, to attend that year's Exotic Ball-Con. Like many people, I collect the mummified nuts of endangered animals, and I had my eye on a cute little pair of penguin testicles that were up for auction at the *Go Nuts!* event in the main conference room. While not strictly an endangered animal, penguins have balls that are harder to come by than the highly sought after nudie calendar *Girls of the Supreme Court 1987*. By the way, I've not had an opportunity to jackoff to that particular piece of memorabilia myself, although I hear the March Sandra Day O'Connor "schoolgirl" spread is really something to see.

In any event, I had been seated on the plane in an exit row and the man-stewardess asked me if I was willing to assist in the event of an emergency. I, of course, said, "Why don't you go fuck yourself," which is apparently something they don't hear a lot. Things got heated, and the pilot finally came out and said something to me about "please put your shirt back on." Eventually, we all calmed down, and he even offered to let me fly the plane a little if I promised to ease up on the whisky. But those were more innocent times.

So there I was standing at the ticket counter at Cuntinental, trying to arrange a seat assignment with the kind of uptight fucker that gives uptight fuckers a bad name. "I'm afraid there are no window or aisle seats left available," the uptight fucker said. "May I recommend that next time you book your seat assignment sooner? *So* sorry." It was the way he said *so* that made me want to dip his nuts in chum and drop him into the Shark Encounter at SeaWorld San Diego so entire families could watch a hammerhead eat his balls.

"Look at me," I replied. "I'm a fat guy. You can't just shove me in the middle seat surrounded by a bunch of dipshits. I won't fit."

"Wish there was something I could do," he replied with a smile that said: "*Cocking you over has made me happier than having my taint licked by coyotes, which is something I greatly enjoy when I'm on vacation with my partner, Toby, in Sedona, Arizona.*" Then he launched into that bullshit spiel about "have you packed your bags yourself and have they been in your possession the whole time?"

"Yeah, yeah, yeah …" I replied until he got to the part about did I have any explosives or firearms in my possession, which made me remember the items I'd picked up on the way to the airport. "Just this dynamite," I said, taking a stick from my jacket.

The prick went pale. "I'm sorry, you have *dynamite* on you?"

"Yeah."

"You were planning to take dynamite on an *airplane?*"

"Yeah. Just in case I might need it later."

His eyes bulged just like a moose's does when you're choking one. "Sir, you cannot bring an explosive on board an airplane."

The girlie hysteria in his voice was starting to feel like a hot needle in my medulla oblongata. "Why not?" I said. "What, you think I'm gonna blow up an airplane with *me on it?* Are you some kind of a retardo?"

"No, I am not a *retardo*, thank you. And you cannot board an airplane with dynamite."

"What's the matter? Don't you trust me?"

You may or may not have realized this by now, but people not trusting me is sort of a pet peeve of mine. The last time it happened, I threatened to ass fuck Obama.

The uptight fucker picked up the phone and started whispering into it. I couldn't hear what he said, but it was clear that he wasn't dictating an article to *Time Magazine* entitled "Jack Icefloe Jackson Is a Super Fucking Guy."

"Put the phone down," I said calmly.

He didn't reply, so I lit the stick of dynamite with my NRA lighter. That seemed to get his attention.

"What are you doing?"

"I'm going to dynamite you to death."

His eyes went as wide as a pussy being parted by a speculum made for fat chicks, and he turned and ran like the girlie he was. I waited for the fuse to burn down before I lobbed the dynamite at him. My years of experience with this particular weapon paid off in spades when it landed just in front of him and blew his head clean off his body. There was a bunch of screaming, and I heard someone yell, "That hick just dynamited Roger!" Before long, cops were swarming all over the place, guns pointed at my head, shouting for me to lay face down on the ground.

"Everyone just relax," I said, reaching into my jacket. That made them do the opposite of relax. I heard what sounded like the cocking of hundreds of weapons. But instead of pulling out a weapon of my own, I pulled out a card. "Take a look at this," I said, holding it up. "I have a license to kill, signed by President Obama, even though I didn't vote for him."

The officer-in-charge walked up and took the card from me. "It's valid," he said, after looking it over. He handed it back, then turned to his men. "Let him go." Everyone lowered their weapons.

"About time," I grunted.

"Sorry to bother you, Mr. Icefloe Jackson," the officer-in-charge said. "We hope you're not too upset. Damn protocol and all."

"No worries," I replied with a shrug. "We'll grab a beer someday and have a laugh about this."

"A cold one sounds good right about now."

"Sure does. Unfortunately, I'm on a mission."

He nodded. "Of course you are. Anything interesting?"

"Just world saving stuff. I'd tell you all about it, but I have a plane to catch, and this asshole was trying to give me the middle seat." I gestured to the remains of the uptight fucker, which were being sponged off the walls.

The officer-in-charge laughed. "You don't need to explain yourself to me. Hell, you have a license to kill. And don't worry, we'll clean up the mess."

"Appreciate it."

I was about to head toward my gate when I saw a little boy crying. He was cute. Blond hair, brown eyes, although I couldn't tell how big his cock was. It was easier to tell with grown men. Something in their eyes let you know whether they were packing a baby gherkin or an elephant trunk.

"What's wrong, kid?" I asked him.

"Why did you kill that man?" he replied in a way that told me if I didn't toughen him up quick, he was going to end up working for Greenpeace.

I turned to his mom. "You mind if I speak to your boy for a moment?"

"Why?" she asked. She looked like she was one prairie dress away from being a Mormon, but I was pretty sure from the way she was eye banging me that her panties were getting as moist as my dead mom's holiday fruitcake.

I gave her my most reassuring smile. "It's just that I think this might be a teachable moment. How old is he, ma'am? Seventeen?"

"Six."

"Oh." Not having children myself, I'd always had difficulties judging their ages. "In any event, I feel he might benefit from my wisdom."

"Well … okay."

"Thanks." I looked down at the kid. "Hello, son. You want to know why I killed that man?" The kid nodded. "Well, I'll tell you, but first you have to answer a question for me. Do you know what a pussy is?"

Thirteen

"UM, NO," THE little kid replied.

"Well, a pussy is the warm, wet thing you find inside of women like your mommy here. It's sort of like the chocolate part of a Hershey's Kiss, and the woman is the foil that you throw away along with that little paper string. Do you understand?"

"Umm," he said. I realized that explaining this was going to be harder than I originally thought. The kid was clearly half retardo.

"Actually, I wish you wouldn't use that word," his mother said.

"Which?"

"The *P-word*."

"What? *Paper*?"

"The other one."

"*Pussy*?"

She looked like she'd just swallowed a cup of pee that smelled like asparagus. "Yes, that one."

No wonder the kid was a mess. He didn't stand a chance with this loon for a mother. "Okay," I said. "Then what do you want me to call it? The only other word I know of for *pussy* is *cun*—"

"NO," she said, cutting me off. Her face looked like the mask from that movie *Scream 2*. "Not that one either. I would prefer that you use the word *vagina*."

I chuckled before I realized she was serious. "Huh?"

"You do know what a vagina is, don't you? It's the clinical term for what you were just talking about."

"What are you, some kind of linguist?"

"No, I ... actually, we really should be going."

I shook my head. "Not just yet. See, I'm trying to educate your boy, because you're obviously not teaching him a goddamn thing worth knowing."

She glanced over at the police, who were putting the ticket agent's head in a bucket. "Okay, hurry please."

I turned back to her kid. "Do you know who the President of the United States is, son?"

"Yes, sir. Obama. My daddy voted for him."

"Well, then your daddy is a shit-flinging assclown but, be that as it may, just a little bit earlier today, Obama asked me to save the world with my cock."

"Wow! Really?" His eyes got wide with excitement.

I nodded. "That's right. See, there's a woman called Pandora who has a pussy so powerful that, if I don't give it the sexy shakes, it's going to turn into a black hole and kill you and your mommy and your stupid shit-flinging Obama-voting daddy. Does that sound like fun to you?"

He shook his head. "No, sir."

"Well, it will *not* be fun, junior. Not by a long shot. Which is why I need to stop it from happening and that guy over there—" I gestured to the ticket clerk, or at least to one of his legs as it was being tagged and wrapped in plastic. "*That* man was trying to impede my progress, so I was forced to dynamite him in the name of national security."

"That's so cool!"

"Fuck, yeah, I am," I said, then shot him a wink. You're welcome, next generation. I headed to my gate. Next stop: New York City and the Bitch Witch.

Fourteen

SERIAL KILLERS PROBABLY think of New York the same way gayboys think of asshole factories—kind of smelly but lots of choices. As I walked through Bloomingdale's heading toward the women's shoe department, I heard the Bitch Witch before I saw her.

"Fuck you, you filthy whore!" she shrieked. "What do you mean you won't buy those pumps? You will buy those fuck-me pumps, or I will pop out your eyeballs and feed them to my kitties!" This was followed by a cackle that sounded a lot like the one the Wicked Witch of the West made in that movie whose name I can never remember.

I rounded the corner to see a tall woman with green skin dressed in a black witch's outfit complete with a pointy black hat. She was looming over a fat chick who was sitting on a chair wearing a pair of red high heeled shoes. The fat chick looked scared.

"But I just don't feel comfortable in them," the fat chick said, unstrapping the shoes, which were dwarfed by her fat feet. She had no more business wearing them than a midget has getting dicked by an elephant. "They don't make me feel pretty."

"Because you *aren't* pretty, you sow!" the Bitch Witch screamed, green spittle flying from her mouth. "You've tried on twenty pairs and bought none of them. You've wasted my precious time, you miserable diseased hippo!"

"You're a very rude lady," the fat chick said, standing to go. "I'm leaving."

"Not without a little *gift*." Cackling, the Bitch Witch took a crusty bottle from a fold in her robe. She unscrewed it and began flinging its thick, milky contents at the woman.

"Stop that!" the fat chick yelled. "It's disgusting."

"It should be. *It's monkey spunk*! I am flinging monkey spunk at you, and now I will curse you. And the curse is this: The next time you shit, you will *shit out your liver*." She laughed maniacally as the fat chick staggered out of the woman's shoe department, eyes wide with shock.

"Oh, dear," a male voice said. I glanced over to see a short guy in a suit hurrying over. He looked like a manager. He seemed worried. "What have you done this time, Bitch Witch?"

The Bitch Witch shrugged. "She was a browser, not a buyer. So I threw monkey spunk on her and cursed her to shit out her liver."

"But you can't *do* that to the customers," he moaned. Sweat popped up on his brow like goose bumps on a naked tit in Greenland. "Now, we've gone over this and over this. If you do it again, I will have to let you go. Do you understand? And please stop flinging monkey spunk at me."

The Bitch Witch was, in fact, flinging monkey spunk at the guy. I liked her for that.

"If you fire me, I will curse you," she said. "And the curse will be this: The next time you piss, acid will shoot from your pecker and your body will melt from the inside until you are nothing but a puddle of slag on a cold hard floor." She cackled again and waved her broom wildly, knocking over a display of suede sandals.

"Oh, Jesus. Forget I said anything," the manager replied. "Just try to keep it down, okay?"

"Maybe!"

He scurried off, leaving the Bitch Witch to start putting shoes back in boxes. I walked over to her.

"Hey, Bitch Witch."

She glanced up at me, and her expression changed instantly. She grinned, but it was not the kind of grin that makes babies laugh. "Jack Icefloe Jackson. I was wondering when you would seek me out."

"You know who I am?"

"Only the finest cocksman that has ever walked on planet Earth."

I nodded. "Guilty as charged. I need your help."

"I know you do. You want to know where to find Pandora, so you can fuck her and make her cuuuuuum." The way she pronounced the word *cum* sort of made you never want to cum again.

"I do," I said. "Do you know where she is?"

The Bitch Witch gave me a lunatic little giggle. "Yes, indeedy. But you are not ready for her, Jack Icefloe Jackson."

"Why not?"

"Because you are not yet *capable* of making her cuuuuuum."

Now it was time for me to chuckle. "Look, Bitch Witch, I made my own *mom* cum when I shot out of her twat during labor. I've given pussy the sexy shakes from Alabama to Antarctica. Hell, I'd even make moon-pussy cum if the moon was only four and a half inches away, which would put it solidly within cock reach. Trust me, I can make this bitch cum."

"You will faaaaaaail!"

"We'll see. Where is she?"

The Bitch Witch sighed, then stared at me with eyes as green and hard as a leper's boner. "Sarah Lawrence University! She's an undergraduate in the Women's Studies department."

Fifteen

SARAH LAWRENCE UNIVERSITY was the most expensive college in the country, so I figured I'd find some pretty pricey pussy there. I wasn't disappointed. Most of the girls acted like their assholes were dipped in diamond dust.

"Hey, you," I said to a thin kid with long hair. He wore a peach-colored backpack that said "Feminists Aren't Always Female," which made about as much sense to me as saying "Motherfuckers Don't Just Fuck their Mothers." Of course, I never went to college, so what the hell do I know? "How can I find Pandora?"

He laughed cheerfully. "Pandora? Why, you can't miss her. Wherever there exists a holy light, an effervescent display of humanity, God's fingerprint on Earth, there you will find Pandora."

Jesus, I wanted to smack him. "Okay, so … where, though? The park? A dorm room? Can you answer me in a way that makes fucking sense?"

He smiled secretively. "You will not find Pandora. She is like a shooting star. She will find *you*."

"Okay. Let me ask you a question, chief. What the hell are you studying here?"

"I am a poetry major, specializing in Pre-Raphaelite haiku."

"Oh."

After I dynamited him to death, I made my way to an area that the students called "Westlands Manor" and I called "big shit-brown building." Out in front, I got my first glimpse of Pandora.

Usually pretty girls surround themselves with warthogs so they look even prettier by comparison. Not Pandora. She was so smoking hot, you didn't even notice the fact that she was surrounded by a six-pack of Victoria's Secret supermodels. She made those sexy bitches look like dung beetles. I feel like I should describe her more to you, but her fuckability was just so off the charts that it's hard to put into words. But I'll try: Giant juggs. Long legs. Tight skirt. Violet eyes. Blond hair so clean and shiny you'd almost feel guilty wiping your cum in it. Hell, she really *was* God's fingerprint on Earth, or whatever the fuck that nerdy poet said about her. In fact, once I realized how impossible it was to describe Pandora *without* poetry, I almost felt bad for blowing the little shit up.

I started walking toward her, thinking about what I was going to say.

Now you might remember that my usual pick-up line is "Open your pussy," but Pandora was in a totally other league, so it seemed like I needed to class it up a little. I stepped up to her and smiled. "Hi, Pandora. Want me to part your beef curtains with my meatstick?"

The supermodels around her swooned, and I could tell by the way they were drooling that they would gladly juggle flaming coals with their tits just for the opportunity to get short-dicked by me, but Pandora did something unexpected. She hauled off and slapped me across the face.

"How dare you speak to me that way!" she said.

I was surprised. She turned out to be much more swanky than I'd realized. It was clear I was going to need to break out some of the fancy words.

"Okay," I said. "What I meant was: Do you want me to pry open your hotbox with my flesh wrench?"

Whack! She slapped me again. I was a little unsure what to do next, and then it came to me. The reason we weren't connecting was that she was an anal girl and my pussy talk held no interest for her. Fine. Anal was my specialty.

"Let me try that again," I said. "My question is: Do you want me to plug your hiney hole with my vein cannon?"

Whack. Again with the damn slap.

"You are the most disgusting man I have ever met," she said.

I noticed she had an accent—British, I think—which meant she wasn't stupid. I sighed. "Alright, maybe I'm beating around the bush too much, so let me try it this way: Do you want me to fuck you? You probably know you've got a world-killing pussy bomb between your legs and, if I don't defuse it soon by making you cum, we're all going to die."

She laughed. "And what makes you think you're the man to defuse this 'bomb'? You're a rather blunt instrument, are you not? And my orgasm response is quite complex. This 'bomb' is beyond your capacity to navigate. It is not simply a question of should you cut the red wire or the blue wire. My vagina has *many* metaphorical wires. Some red, some blue, some indigo, some azure, some are even cerulean. You are quite incapable of handling it. Trust me."

"Wow. You're really making me not want to fuck you."

"Go away, you fat, bald, repulsive little man. Go away and never return."

She walked past me then, and I felt a strange emotion, one I'd never felt before.

Rejection.

Sixteen

I'M ASHAMED TO say that I did not handle it well.

Most guys have some experience with bitches not wanting to fuck them, but not me. Actually, it had happened once before but that's because it turned out the woman had malaria and wasn't medically capable of wanting to fuck me at the time, although she did give me a handjob. Point is, Pandora's rejection shook me so badly that I decided to become celibate for a few hours and go on a bender.

I had a powerful thirst for moonshine, which meant I needed to find a hick. The hick that lived on the outskirts of Sarah Lawrence University was a guy named Jebadiah Barnes. He made his home in a tree by a drainage culvert where he amused himself by jacking off on the unsuspecting joggers who ran beneath. He had a jug full of moonshine made from cactus juice that he gladly shared with me. I drank myself blind.

Eventually, I ended up semi-conscious in the drainage culvert staring up at Jebadiah in his tree as he feverishly stroked his cock like a retard in a lunchroom, trying his damnedest to rain cum down on me. That was a low point. I passed out. And that's when Obama came to me in a dream.

"What the hell are you doing, Icefloe?" Obama said.

"I have been rejected by a bitch, so now I'm drinking myself to death while a monkey man jacks off on me."

Obama shook his head sadly. "You can't let it end like this. I need you. The *world* needs you. You have to pick yourself up, dust yourself off and get this thing done."

"How? Pandora said I was fat and bald, which should have gotten her pussy wetter than an Amazonian rain forest. I don't understand. What's happening to me?"

Obama sat down on a boulder. "It's simple, really. You're afraid of the pussy."

"Come on."

"I'm serious. It happened to me once. After I became president, I had an enormous problem being intimate with my wife. On the night of the inauguration, I lay in bed with her absolutely petrified."

"Why?"

"Because I realized that I was no longer dealing with regular pussy. Now I was dealing with *first lady* pussy, and that's a horse of a different color my friend."

Him saying "horse of a different color" reminded me of that horse of a different color that lived in the Emerald City with the Wizard of Oz from that movie whose name I can never remember. I nodded. "I hear you. So what did you do?"

"I realized that circumstances had fundamentally *changed* and that I needed to change with them. And that may be what you need to do, Icefloe. Change a little, just like I did. Eventually, I was able to make love to my wife again."

"To make what?"

"To fuck her."

"Oh."

Obama stood. "You're going to be fine, Icefloe. I changed and so can you. Now go back to Manhattan and visit the Bitch Witch in her hovel. And be humble this time. Let her tell you what you need to do, how you need to change—and then do it. Okay?"

"Okay."

Obama looked skyward. "And if you cum on me, Jebadiah, I will yank you from that tree and skull fuck you."

Jebadiah grunted and put his cock back in his pants as the President walked off. I was beginning to like that Obama. He had some balls on him. I sobered up and then headed back to the Bitch Witch.

Seventeen

FROM THE OUTSIDE, the Bitch Witch's apartment looked like a typical brownstone on the Upper East Side, but inside it was a medieval hovel, a hellhole crammed with gutted snakes hanging from rafters, jars full of eyeballs and a bubbling cauldron that was filled with a thick brown liquid that smelled strongly of goat anus. The Bitch Witch used a wooden paddle to stir it as I entered.

"Hiya, Bitch Witch."

"Jack Icefloe Jackson," she cackled. "I knew you would return. So tell me ... did you fuck Pandora? Did you bring her to orrrrrgasm?" I liked hearing her pronounce *orgasm* even less than I liked hearing her pronounce *cum*.

"You know I didn't," I said. "She wouldn't even give me a shot at giving her the sexy shakes."

She cackled again. "Told you, didn't I? I said you were not ready. But did you listen? *Nooooooo.*"

"Well, I'm listening now. Obama came to me in a dream and said to talk to you and be humble. So what do I need to do?"

She stopped stirring the pot and threw in a couple toads. "You see, the problem is that Pandora is not like other girls. She is a *real woman*. Which means you must do more than satisfy her sexually."

That sort of stumped me. "What do you mean? What else is there aside from open pussy, insert cock?"

"If you are to make Pandora cuuuuuum, you must also satisfy her spiritually and emotionally and intellectually."

I let out a long, low whistle. "What the *fuck*?"

"Saving the world takes work. You must stretch, Jack Icefloe Jackson. You must grow. You must *change* if you are to complete this awesome task. You must become … *a sensitive man*."

That's when I knew she was full of shit. "Look, bitches don't want sensitivity. They want a hard cock wielded by a guy who knows how to operate it."

The Bitch Witch spit angrily in the kettle. "You have tried that and you have failed. Listen to me. You must do exactly what I tell you if the human race is to survive."

I sighed. "Hey, I got an idea. Why don't you and I go make fucky fucky? Your face is as ugly as the shitstains on my drawers, but it looks like you got a smoking hot body under that robe. It'll take our minds off things."

"Never," she shrieked. "I am a witch! I must remain untouched, for if any man enters my unholiest of unholies, it will cause a lunar eclipse that will plunge the Earth into endless winter." She shook her head. "No, Jack Icefloe Jackson, you must focus on making *Pandora* cum or her vajayjay will turn into a black hole and destroy us all."

"Man, there's a lot of complicated pussy out there."

She nodded. "No shit, Sherlock."

I took a breath and strengthened my resolve. "Okay. I need to be a sensitive guy. Got it. I need to learn how to satisfy Pandora emotionally and—what were those other things?"

"Spiritually and intellectually."

"Right. Jesus, what a pain in the ass. So how do I go about doing all that?"

She leaned in so close that I could see a spider laying eggs on her scalp. "You will be taught, Jack Icefloe Jackson. You will receive lessons in sensitivity by the greatest instructors of our age. First, we begin with your spiritual training. And for that, you must go to the Vatican and seek out *the Hot Nuns of Assisi!*"

Eighteen

THE VATICAN WAS packed with tourists as I walked through St. Peter's Square on my way to meet the Pope. I didn't have an appointment, but I figured he'd want to talk to me seeing as how I was trying to save the world. A flock of cardinals walked by dressed in their signature stupid red outfits topped off with those ridiculous red beanies.

"Hey, cardinals," I said. They all turned and stared at me. It was like looking at a shelf of ketchup bottles. "I need to talk to the Pope. Where is he?" No answer. It was like they'd all taken a vow of shut-the-fuck-up, but what they didn't know was that I'd taken a vow of I-don't-give-a-shit.

"Someone better start talking," I said. "I'm trying to save the world here, which means I gotta get sensitive and to do that I gotta hook up with the Hot Nuns of Assisi."

The cardinals glanced at each other. I had struck a nerve. One of them, an old fuck with a whisky nose, stepped forward. He talked with a Catholic accent. "There is no such thing as the Hot Nuns of Assisi, my son."

"You're lying, Padre," I said. "Take me to them."

"I'm afraid you are mistaken." His eyes were as cold as the marble cock on the statue of David. "Good day to you. May God bless you and keep you safe."

He turned to go and the rest of the cardinals followed.

"Okay," I said, taking out a stick of dynamite. "I guess you want to do this the hard way."

I lit the fuse and began lobbing dynamite across St. Peter's Square. There were massive explosions, one after another, and the cardinals went airborne just like the birds they were named after. People screamed and shouted, and I heard someone yelling: "That lunatic is dynamiting the cardinals!" Within seconds, the Vatican police arrived, pointing weapons at me and screaming in Italian.

"Hey, hey, hey," I said. "Speak English already. I can't understand a word you're saying. All I hear is 'spaghetti, spaghetti, fettucine, ravioli.'"

The head of the Vatican police stepped forward. "You are to stop lighting dynamite and put your hands up, yes? You are under arrest, yes?"

"No," I said, taking a card from my pocket. "See, I'm on a mission to save the world. Plus, I got this license to kill here, signed by Obama."

He took the card and looked at it. "It's valid," he said to his men. The police lowered their weapons. "We're very sorry to trouble you, sir. Come back and visit us any time, yes? And don't worry, we'll mop up the cardinals for you."

"Thanks, but I'm afraid I can't leave until I learn how to get sensitive—which I can only do by meeting with the Hot Nuns of Assisi."

"Impossible." He glanced around, then leaned in close to me and whispered, "Only the Pope himself can authorize a visit with the Hot Nuns."

"So you admit they exist? Then it looks like I need to talk to the Pope."

"That is, I'm afraid, out of the question. No one is allowed to meet with the pontiff." He folded his arms across his chest.

"Okay. So it's back to the dynamite then?" I took another stick from my coat. "Fine by me."

I flicked open my lighter when a Pope-y voice boomed across the square: "*Wait.*" I looked up to see an old man in a fucked-up hat standing on a balcony. It was the Pope. "No more blowing people up, my son. I will meet with you."

Nineteen

"THE HOT NUNS of Assisi are the Vatican's most precious secret," the Pope said as we sat in his office, drinking papal beer. It was watery, like his eyes. "Nuns, of course, take a vow of celibacy," the Pope continued. "But *these* nuns, they are so beautiful that no man could resist them, so we must keep them locked away in a hidden chamber deep below St. Peter's Square for their own protection."

"You dirty old pig," I said, smiling. "You got your own little harem, don't you? The Best Little Whorehouse in the Vatican."

"*Nein*," the Pope said. I couldn't tell if he was German or just liked Hitler talk. "I do not partake of the Hot Nuns, nor does anyone. They are virgins. Untouched. Stroked only by God!" His face had grown flushed, either from alcohol or creepy jack-off thoughts of the Hot Nuns.

"Relax," I said. "I didn't mean to get you so stirred up. Jesus. So, when you say only *God* strokes the nuns, what do you mean by that exactly?"

"Well, in the Catholic church, we believe that the nuns are actually married to God."

"So you're saying God's a polygamist? He's got a lot of wives?" The Pope made a sort of grinchy face. "What's the matter?" I asked. "Hemorrhoids?"

"No."

"It's okay. You can tell me. Hell, we all get 'em from time to time. There's no shame in it."

"I said, it's not hemorrhoids."

"I can recommend a cream."

"It's not hemorrhoids, dammit!" the Pope yelled. "And God is not a polygamist, either!"

I raised my hands. "Fine. Okay. *Whatever*. Let's just get right to it. I need to meet with these bitches."

The Pope cocked an eyebrow. "Excuse me?"

"The nuns? The Hot Nuns of Assisi?"

"Ah." He shook his head. "Impossible, I'm afraid. No men are allowed to see them. Not even *I* have seen them. They are attended to only by women, who we must constantly replace because the Hot Nuns are so hot they eventually turn them all into lesbians—which the Catholic Church does not condone."

"Okay, then let me lay it on the line for you: I need them to help me save the world from a pussy that's going to turn into a planet-destroying black hole if I don't fuck it good enough."

The Pope went ashen. "You speak of Pandora."

"You heard of her?"

He nodded. "She has been foretold since biblical times. She is fated to be the bringer of the apocalypse, the end of the world."

"I know what the fuck *apocalypse* means."

"I'm sorry, what?"

"I may look like a hick but I know what the fuck *apocalypse* means. You don't have to define it. Christ, how stupid do you think I am?"

"Apologies." He smoothed out his robe, then popped the cap off another bottle of beer and handed it to me. "Please, have more papal beer. We brew it in the Basilica."

I waved him off. "No thanks. So about the Hot Nuns ..."

He nodded. "I will arrange it. I don't understand exactly how they are supposed to help you, but your quest is just. If they can be of service, I will see to it that you meet them."

"Thanks. And I'm sorry for snapping at you just now."

"It's quite alright."

I was actually starting to warm up to the Pope. He wasn't really such a bad guy. "Hey, do you collect the balls of endangered species by any chance?"

"No."

"It's a great hobby. Tell you what, I'm gonna start you off by sending you some dried penguin testicles. They're very hard to come by. Penguin balls are *tiny*."

"That's really not necessary."

"Of course it's not necessary," I said. "It's a gift. Gifts are never *necessary*, like blowjobs or ass play. Hey, do you have kids?"

The Pope shook his head. "No. I am the Pope."

"Well, that's too bad because kids really like penguin testicles. Hey, you want to know what funny thought just came into my head?"

"Okay."

"I bet when French guys yell out 'Pope' to you, it sounds like this: '*Poop, Poop.*' You know, because of the accent?"

He nodded. "Yes, I can see how that would be funny."

It didn't look to me like he could see how it would be funny. In fact, it didn't look to me like he found *anything* all that funny, which was too bad. "You don't laugh a lot, do you?" I said. "You know, you should laugh more. Truth is, when guys in your position don't laugh, they end up starting wars and killing people."

"That's very profound."

I shrugged. I knew it was. "Hey, do you want to play a game? It's fun."

The Pope glanced at his watch. "I'm sorry, I really can't. I have to say mass."

"Come on, it'll be quick." I turned away from him and, when I turned back, I pointed to my unzipped fly. My right hand was down there, and I showed the Pope a little patch of skin I was pinching between my thumb and forefinger. "Cock or balls?" I asked.

The Pope seemed confused. "I'm sorry, I'm not following."

"This little piece of skin I'm showing you, is it from my cock or from my balls?"

"I ... I don't know. It is very hard to tell."

I nodded. "Yeah, that's what makes it such a good game. Go on, take a guess."

The Pope leaned forward and inspected my crotch. "I don't know. I don't see much hair on it so I'm going to say ... cock? No, balls!"

"You sure?"

"I don't know."

"Look more closely. Pay attention to the texture of the skin. Does it have dimples?"

He squinted. "Yes, it does. Which means it's balls! *Definitely balls.*"

"Bingo! Which is probably a game you're a little more familiar with. Am I right or am I right?"

The Pope allowed a small grin. "I admit I've spun the basket a time or two."

"I knew it." I zipped up and then shook his hand. "Well, nice to meet you. And I really appreciate you helping me out."

"You're quite welcome. By the way, you mentioned a cream earlier …"

"Hemorrhoid cream?" The Pope gave me an embarrassed little nod. "I knew you needed it. Like I said, we all get them. No shame in it. I'll write it down for you." I wrote "*Preparation H—Walgreens has it*" on the upper right corner of the open Gutenberg Bible on the Pope's desk. "There you go, Chief."

"Thank you, my son. You are quite a man, Jack Icefloe Jackson."

I clapped him on the back. "Tell me something I don't know. Now, take me to those Hot Nuns. It's time to get sensitive."

Twenty

THE HOT NUNS of Assisi were bathing each other in a spring fed pool hidden away in a secret chamber underneath St. Peter's Square. They were all nude except for the headpieces of their habits. Every one of them was a smoking hot 10 or, in church numbers, an X. I stood there a moment checking them out, until the sexiest one of them walked up to me, droplets of water clinging to her perfect nips.

"You must be Jack Icefloe Jackson," she said. "We were told to expect you."

"Well, I'm here," I replied. "I got some world saving to do, and a woman called the Bitch Witch thought you could help."

She nodded. "We will certainly do all we can. My name is Mother Superior Honeypot. I am the head of the order of the Hot Nuns of Assisi. I was told to help you achieve a spiritual awakening."

"Well, you've certainly helped me achieve a *cock* awakening. Man, I can't stop looking at your tits. I swear, those are probably the best juggs I've ever seen on a nun."

She blushed. "Thank you. And I'm sorry I'm distracting you

with them. I've never seen a man before, so I didn't realize how appealing you might find my perfect tight teenage body. Would you prefer I cover myself up?"

I shook my head. "Nah. We should keep those great juggs exposed to moisture. Don't want 'em to dry out. Get all leathery."

"Quite sensible." She took me by the hand and led me to a velvet couch with the same ease as a stripper bringing a guy to the VIP lounge for a little slap and tickle. "So, shall we talk about spirituality?" she asked.

"Sure."

She leaned in close, and I was pretty sure she was either going to ask me something really serious or blow me. It turned out she wasn't looking to blow me. "Do you believe in God, Mr. Icefloe Jackson?"

I laughed at the obviousness of the question. "Hell yeah. I mean, pussy didn't make itself, now did it?"

Her big blue eyes widened. "That's quite a curious take on the subject."

"Speaking of curious takes, I'm curious how you take care of that firm ass of yours. Pilates? Do you use body butter?"

She shook her head. "I don't do anything unusual. I'm just as God made me. So let's talk about religion. Do you consider yourself a member of any particular one?"

I shrugged. "Not really. I like bits and pieces of all of them. To me, picking a religion is kind of like ordering off a Chinese menu. A little something from column A, a little something from column B. Which reminds me: Do you know why I like fucking Chinese bitches?"

She shook her head.

"Well, it's because they so horn—ah, forget it. You probably wouldn't understand. But my point is that I enjoy different things about different religions. For instance, you Catholics drink like fish, which I love. Jews don't believe in Hell, which is probably good for me in the long run. And Scientologists figured out a way to make religion fun. They turned it into a video game, with space aliens and different levels. So, I guess I'd have to say that I think of myself as being a member of all of them, sort of a Scien-jew-olic."

Mother Superior stared at me. "You are quite an unusual man, Mr. Icefloe Jackson."

"I *am* unique."

"Let's talk about faith. What is your position on faith?"

"I'd fuck her," I said. "I mean, I don't know what *position* I'd use. Maybe doggy style?" Mother Superior Honeypot narrowed her eyes, and I realized I'd come close to making what the Greeks call a faux pas. "You're not talking about Faith Mayfield, my old elementary school teacher, are you?"

Honeypot shook her head.

"Sorry, I misunderstood. Yeah, old Faith Mayfield would have to be in her sixties by now, but I bet she's still bangable. She had a rack you could land a lunar module on."

Honeypot cleared her throat. "Why don't we just move on? Tell me, have you read the Bible?"

I nodded. "From cover to cover, particularly the jack-off material."

"Excuse me?"

I didn't want to say anything inappropriate, so I whispered the next part to her: "You know ... about the *whores*."

"Oh. Right. I guess I was mostly curious if there any particular *stories* in the Bible that spoke to you?"

I nodded. "Of course. In fact, one of them changed my whole view on employment. It's the story of Job, who was this guy who was actually *named* Job, and a ton of truly horrible shit happens to him, which was God's way of saying, 'If you get a job, bad shit will happen to you,' which is why I've never had a job in my entire life." I leaned back, satisfied.

She stared at me a long time. "I believe it's pronounced *Jobe*," she said finally. "With a long *O*."

"Then why is it spelled *Job*?"

"I don't know. I suppose that's just how they spelled things in those days."

"Huh. Man, you got great tits. So are we going to fuck or what?"

She seemed a little taken aback. "No, certainly not. Why would we?"

"I don't know. It's just, if we're not gonna fuck, I don't exactly know what I'm *doing* here. I mean, I'm not feeling any more sensitive or spiritual or anything. Hey, what is that nun doing with that cucumber?"

"Eyes on me, please," the Mother Superior said, snapping her fingers in front of my face. "I can see that this isn't working. I shall have to try harder."

"Okay."

She did her best. For hours, she talked to me about how you could see God's face in a flower and how your heart was a vessel you could fill with love but, truth be told, I just couldn't stop staring at her tits. When she talked, all I heard coming out of those sweet red nun lips was "blah, blah, blah."

Finally, she gave up. "I don't know what to do, Mr. Icefloe Jackson. I have explained the wonders of spirituality to you in every way I know how, and yet you still do not seem to understand."

I shrugged. "It's not your fault. I've always been a bad student. Truth is, book learning has never been my strong suit. I learn better by *doing*."

She thought about that a moment and, when she turned back to me, I could see that she'd come to a life-changing decision. "With the world hanging in the balance, there is perhaps only one way I can make you understand. If you learn by doing, then I must *do you*. I must make love to you, Jack Icefloe Jackson. I must school you in the mysteries of the spiritual world using only my vagina."

"Now we're talking."

She climbed onto my meatpole and rode me so hard that I actually did see the face of God. He was good looking in a Mexican way, like Ricardo Montalban. And when Mother Superior Honeypot climaxed, all of her spiritual beliefs shot out of her pussy, down my dick and into my soul where it filled me with love and joy. I finally understood what the hell she'd been talking about for the last five hours.

Unfortunately, right then, a beam of white light shot down from heaven and consumed her. She turned into ash and crumbled all over me. But, just before she did, I gave her a compliment to take with her into the afterlife.

"Hey babe," I said. "That was really great. Fucking you was like taking not-angry pills."

"Thank you," she replied, and then she was gone.

Filled with all this new spirituality, I headed back to the Bitch Witch.

Twenty-One

I ENTERED THE Bitch Witch's hovel to find her sitting on a food-stained couch watching a black-and-white TV. "Well, if it isn't Jack Icefloe Jackson," she said while stroking the filthy cat on her lap. Her hand came up dirty.

"Sure is," I said with a nod. "What's all that shit on your face?" It was covered in green goo, like she'd been cummed on by a leprechaun.

"It's a moisturizing mask. I like to do one while I watch *Wheel*."

A crowd of people on the TV shouted, "Wheel! Of! Fortune!" Then the Bitch Witch spoke along with the announcer, "Look at these *fabulous* prizes …"

I sighed. "So this is what you do all day when I'm not around? Watch crappy game shows and put green shit on your face?"

"Oh, shut up. I have to have *some* fun. It's not exactly as if the blue bird of happiness is roosting in my fucking hovel." She threw the cat off her lap. "So how did it go? Did you hook up with the Hot Nuns of Assisi?"

I nodded. "Sure did. And I banged one of them and became spiritual. I have to say, it was really sort of life changing.

I'd always believed in God but never like this. It's hard to explain, but I learned that we are all equal in the eyes of the Lord. Together, we make up a glorious tapestry of humanity. Death is not the end of our journey, it's the beginning of a new one. Also, God is love."

"Oh, you insufferable cunt." She spit disgustedly on the floor. "I liked you much better the way you were before—godless and ignorant."

"Hey, I'm trying to fuck an unusual pussy, here. You think I *like* being like this? We all have to edge out of our comfort zones."

"I know, I know ..."

I heard a faint tapping sound from somewhere in the next room. "What's that?" I asked.

She looked away. "Nothing. Rats in the pipes. Why don't we get you going on your next task so that you can learn to become even *more* sensitive?"

"Okay. Although I wouldn't mind some dinner first." Something smelled good in her apartment, which was unusual considering it normally smelled like goat anus. "I'm actually pretty hungry. I worked up quite an appetite banging that nun."

She shook her head, causing her pointy black witch cap to bob violently. "Sorry, I don't have enough food. And you really should be going."

Tap-tap-tap. More insistent now.

"That's coming from the oven," I said, brushing past the Bitch Witch and entering the kitchen. I walked up to the cast iron stove.

"Get away from that!" she shrieked. "Don't you open it. It's private. What's in there is my business."

Tap-tap-tap. Louder now.

"What in God's name do you have in here?" I said and then

yanked open the oven door. A beautifully cooked ham shank was inside, roasting in its own juices. It wasn't what I was expecting. "Huh. A ham."

"Yes, a ham. Why not?"

"I don't know, I just … I didn't picture you cooking a ham."

"Why? What did you *think* I was cooking? A kid?" I turned away from her so she couldn't see the guilty expression on my face. The Bitch Witch's eyes went wide. "Wait a minute. You *were* thinking that, weren't you? That's exactly what you thought!"

"Don't be ridiculous. I mean … hell, I don't know. I heard tapping …"

"You thought I was cooking a kid!" She cackled so hard that she actually had to grip the side of the oven to keep from falling over. "That's unbelievable. What do you think? That I live in a fucking Grimm's fairy tale?"

"How the hell should I know what you eat? Last time I was here, you were cooking a pot of goat anus soup."

"Because goat anus soup is delicious!" Then, in a high pitched voice, she yelled, "Hansel? Gretel? *Where are you, children?* Come into my candy house so I can eat you …"

"Alright, just stop it. Don't be a dick."

"Nibbling, nibbling like a mouse," she continued, howling with laughter. "Who's that nibbling at my house?"

"Ha ha, very funny."

Tap-tap-tap.

"Damn, there's that sound again," I said. "What *is* that?" It wasn't coming from the oven, I realized. It was coming from the closet. I walked over to it.

"Wait!" the Bitch Witch said, sprinting toward me. "Don't

open that door. *Seriously.*"

I opened it. Sitting on the floor of the closet was a little kid in an aluminum pan, trussed up like a Thanksgiving turkey. He had an apple stuffed in his mouth. "Son of a bitch, you *were* planning to cook a kid!" I yelled. "I knew it!"

"Oh, so what? Give me a break. I'm a fucking witch, alright? This is just the kind of shit I do."

"What about the sanctity of life?"

"Says Mr. Look-at-Me-I'm-All-Spiritual-Now. Don't be such a fucking hypocrite. If this had happened yesterday, you'd be asking for the white meat."

"You're out of your mind." I yanked the little boy out of the closet. "Don't worry, kid. You're gonna be okay."

"What a fucking hero you are," the Bitch Witch said. "Dudley Do-Right." She took the apple out of the kid's mouth and cut the ropes that bound him. "Now go home, you little shit. But if you tell anyone I tried to eat you, I will cook you and your family and your puppies and your goldfishes! Got it?"

The kid nodded and ran off.

I shook my head. "You're terrible."

"And hungry now, because of you."

"Then let's go get some Chinese food. See, I like going to Chinese restaurants because they're filled with Chinese bitches and I like to fuck Chinese bitches because—"

"They so horny, I know, I know. Would you get a new goddamn line already? You're boring the hell out of me with that one."

"Man, you *are* bitchy."

"It's been a long day, and I want to get out of this moisturizing mask. Look, let me just send you on the next leg of your journey of self discovery, okay?"

I nodded, although I wasn't happy with her pissy attitude. "Fine."

"So here's where we're at," she said. "You learned how to relate to women on a spiritual level. Now you must learn to relate to them on an *intellectual* level."

"And who teaches that bullshit?" I asked with a sigh. "Some kind of stupid philosopher chick?"

"No, smart-ass. *The smoking hot secret bastard granddaughter of Albert Einstein!*"

Twenty-Two

AMBER EINSTEIN RAN the proton collider at Hangar 18, the Department of Defense's top-secret weapons facility in the Nevada desert. Her IQ was said to be in the three hundred range, but it was hard to tell because of how crippled she was. She was in one of those Stephen Hawking wheelchairs, and she couldn't move her arms or legs or head, but she had a body on her that would give a baby a boner. She used her tongue to manipulate a joystick that controlled her wheelchair as well as the weird voice machine that talked for her. As soon as I walked into her lab, she rolled up to me and started speaking like a robot.

"Jack. Icefloe. Jackson. I. Have. Been. Expecting. You."

"Yeah. Uh, nice to meet you."

"I. Have. Been. Told. To. Assist. You. In. Learning. To. Communicate. Intellectually. With. A. Wom—"

I waved my hand in front of her face. "Let me just stop you there. No offense, but that creepy voice just isn't working for me. I mean, it's not even a little bit sexy. It's not making my cock heavy *at all*."

"It. Is. Not. Supposed. To. Make. Your. Cock. Heavy."

Her face didn't really move, so it was hard to tell if she was aggravated or not. Just to be safe, I decided to pour on the charm. I gave her my best smile. "What I mean is, there's probably a better setting on that thing. Some other voice that might turn me on a little more. Let me take a look." I fiddled around with her mouth computer and discovered that there were a bunch of voices you could choose from. I picked *Porn Star—Female*. "Here, try this one."

She started speaking, and the voice that came out now was completely different. "But I don't *want* to sound like a porn star—" she said, sounding just like a porn star.

"Now that's more like it." Her new voice was so hot and sexy you could almost hear "Bow Chicka Wow Wow" music in the background. And then I realized that there was no *almost* about it. The machine actually supplied porn star music every time she spoke.

"I hate this voice," she said. *Chicka, chicka, bow-wooooow!*

"Listen to me," I said. "Just because you're all handicapped doesn't mean you can't be a sexy ass bitch, too."

"I'm not handicapped. I'm handicapable." *Waa-Waaaaaa! Chicka …*

"Handicapable?" I said. "Hell, you're not even capable of *raising* your hand. Nope, you're handicapped, alright. But you're also smoking hot and, just so you know, I'd gladly slip you a few inches—and not just out of pity." I shot her a reassuring wink. Sometimes bitches needed to be treated tenderly.

She sighed in a way that might have been kind of angry, although it was hard to tell because the machine made it sound like she was cumming. She continued talking. "Alright, let's just get on with this. Tell me about your experiences dealing with intelligent women. What do you talk to them about?"

"Talk with who?"

"Women. Smart women."

"Right. Who?"

"Intelligent women. Brainy women."

I was having trouble understanding her. Maybe it was all that porn star music in the background. "Hang on," I said. "You mean women with great big juggs?"

"No, you're misunderstanding me." She almost sounded like she was getting frustrated, but I wasn't sure. "Let me try again," she said. "I just want to know what kind of conversations you have with women of intellect."

"Ah, okay." I thought about that a second. "What are we talking about?"

"Intelligent women," she repeated. I noticed that her eyes were starting to bulge a little, which wasn't sexy at all.

"Okay. But before I answer that, let me ask you this: Are we joking now, or is this part of the actual lesson?"

"No, we are not fucking joking," she said. "I just want to know how you talk to smart women because smart women like to be with smart men."

"Sorry, say that again? And this time, please ask your question using the kinds of words that actually convey what you mean."

"Jesus Christ," she shouted. "I just want to know how do you talk to women, you fucking idiot!" The porn music hit a hysterical crescendo. *Boom-boom-chicka-boom-boom-POW!*

It was sad, really. For such a supposed smart bitch she was absolutely incapable of forming an intelligible thought. Her pulse was hooked up to a beeping monitor that was starting to beep like crazy. She tried to calm herself down with some sort of breathing technique. The beeping slowed.

Finally, she spoke again. "Okay, why don't we try a different approach?"

"Sounds good."

"Let's investigate your general knowledge on a range of

subjects. Being the secret bastard daughter of Albert Einstein, my specialty is physics. So why don't we begin with that? Do you know the meaning of the formula $E=MC^2$?"

I nodded. "Of course. Who doesn't? It's fucking famous."

"Good," she said. "Then we can move on …" She paused a moment, then continued: "Actually, just to satisfy my curiosity, can you explain to me what $E=MC^2$ stands for?"

"Sure. It's a formula for getting a hard-on."

"Ah, there we go. I'm glad we turned over this rock. Can you elaborate please?"

I shrugged. "If you want. E stands for erection. M is masturbation and C is, obviously, cunt. And cunt squared means lots of cunts. So $E=MC^2$ means masturbation while thinking about multiple cunts equals an erection."

I think if she was capable of shaking her head, she would have. "My God. I would dearly love to put your brain in a petri dish, dissect it and scan it thoroughly. I believe we would discover something unprecedented."

"Hell, yeah," I said. "I'm nothing if not unprecedented. Now go on. Give me another famous formula."

"Alright. Do you know the meaning of *pi*?"

"Yeah, but I doubt you want to hear it."

"Try me."

I shrugged. "Okay. *Pie* is short for *hair pie*. Which is a metaphor for pussy, made famous by a shitty movie called *American Pie*, which is about a kid fucking a pie, which feels to him like he's fucking a pussy, which is where we get the term *pie*. What do you think it is?"

"Well, *I* would have said it's a mathematical constant whose value is the ratio of any circle's circumference to its diameter in

Euclidean space, but your metaphor for pussy idea is interesting, too."

"Different strokes, I guess."

She seemed eager to leave the world of physics behind her, so we decided to give art a shot. "Are you familiar with the *Mona Lisa?*" she asked.

"You mean the most famous painting the world? Sure, I'm familiar with the *Moaning Lisa*. In fact, I even have a theory about what old Lisa's moaning about."

"Let me guess. Your penis?"

I shook my head. "Don't be ridiculous. I wasn't even *born* when that painting was painted. Nope, I believe she's moaning because she's enjoying a vibrating anal egg." I paused to let that sink in, then I elaborated: "See, that's the reason she's got that secretive little half-smile. It's because she's got a vibrating egg inserted into her anus."

That ended the art discussion.

We tried a couple more categories, but nothing I said seemed to make Amber Einstein happy. In fairness to me, most of this stuff doesn't come up in regular conversation, and I'm even pretty certain she got some of it wrong. For instance, she kept insisting that the famous philosopher quote, "I think, therefore I'm man" was something totally different, although I'll spot her that it was come up with by a dude named Descartes, whoever the fuck *he* is. In any event, I felt kind of bad that I couldn't seem to satisfy Amber intellectually, mostly because I knew this was heading nowhere good.

"I don't know what to do," she said finally. If she could have moved her arms, I know she'd have thrown them in the air in frustration. "I understand that the fate of the world is hanging in the balance, but I simply cannot figure out how to make you an intellectual."

"I was afraid of this," I said. "I had the same problem with Mother Superior Honeypot, the head of the order of the Hot Nuns of Assisi. She was trying to make me spiritual, and she ran into a brick wall, too. Although, after what she did, now I'm filled with the glory of the infinite, and my capacity to both give and receive love is dwarfed only by my feelings for God's blessed gift of humankind."

"That's amazing," Amber said. "How did she do that? How did Mother Superior Honeypot achieve such a miracle?"

"Well, she fucked me, and when she came, all that spirituality shot out of her pussy, down my dick and into my soul."

"And that actually worked?"

I nodded. "Yup."

"Huh. And are you now suggesting that I do the same?"

I shrugged. "Well, I think that's likely the only thing that's going to make me super smart, but there's a glitch to the plan. See, it actually killed Honeypot. She died right after she came. Now, I'm not saying the same thing will happen to you but … you gotta factor that in."

Amber Einstein seemed to think for a long time. Finally, she said, "I must do it, even at risk to my own life. After all, the needs of the many outweigh the needs of the few."

"Did Descartes say that?"

"No, Spock. But it's quite apt, don't you think?"

"I guess."

Amber smiled sadly, or would have if she could have moved her face. "Let's just get this over with."

Now, I'm a modest man, so I don't want to give you too many details about the unbelievable sex that followed. But when the only thing you can move during your entire lifetime is your tongue, that tongue learns to do some shit you can't even find on the Internet. Amber Einstein rocked my world. When we were done, she came super hard. And all her smarts shot out of her pussy, down my dick and into my brain, filling me with all kinds of intellectual thoughts.

"That was incredible, Icefloe!" she said, using her own voice for the first time in her life while clapping her hands in ecstasy. For a moment, I thought that maybe my cock had cured her paralysis, and now she was going to be able to walk and talk again. But, nope, she died.

I was sad to see her go.

She was a good one, Amber Einstein. And even though she was really smart, she was also *nice*—which is rare. Ralph Waldo Emerson probably said it best: "Character is higher than intellect. A great soul will be strong to live as well as think."

I like that, don't you?

Cogito ergo sum, motherfucker.

Twenty-Three

I RETURNED TO New York to discover that the Bitch Witch had gone back to work in the women's shoe department at Bloomingdale's. Once again, I heard her before I saw her as I made my way through the brightly lit aisles, fragrant with perfume.

"You will buy those patent leather Mary Janes," she shrieked, "or I'll smack you in your stupid face with a baboon's liver!"

I rounded a handbag display to see the Bitch Witch in her familiar black robe, jabbing an elderly lady with the butt end of her broomstick.

"But they're two sizes too small," the old woman complained. "I can't feel my feet."

"That's because you've got diabetes, you cow. Just take your insulin and shut the fuck up!"

Her manager paced in the background. He looked worried. "Excuse me, Bitch Witch?" he said. "Could I have a word?"

"Not now."

"But it's very important."

"Not now, you ass. I am *with a customer.*"

"Okay, then," he said, scurrying away.

"I had best be going," the old woman said as she struggled to remove the too-tight shoes with a pained expression on her face.

The Bitch Witch waved her broom threateningly. "You're not going *anywhere*, you sow, until you buy those Mary Janes!"

The situation was growing desperate. I walked up to two of them. "Hey there, Bitch Witch."

She glanced over at me. "Oh, hi, Icefloe. I'll be with you in a moment."

I kneeled down and took a look at the old lady's feet. "You know, I think she's right—those shoes *are* too tight for her."

"So what? What are you, a fucking cobbler now? We don't have them in her size. Jesus Christ, leave me alone, Icefloe. I'm trying to make a goddamn sale here."

She seemed even bitchier than usual. I was going to have to tread carefully. "I understand that you want to close a sale," I said, "but a woman this age is likely to have arthritis, which is a condition that can be worsened by ill-fitting shoes. This kind of musculoskeletal problem is painful and, if not properly taken care of, can force the need for arthroplasty. She already lacks an adequate amount of synovial fluid in her joints, so let's not exacerbate the problem with inappropriate shoes."

"Oh, shut up, you cunt. I take it from all your fancy ten-dollar words that you visited Amber Einstein?"

I nodded. "She's dead now, but she filled me with her vast intellect before she passed. It's a damn shame she's gone. I really liked her."

"Boo fucking hoo. Why do you even give a shit? Aren't you filled with the *spirit* now after banging Mother Superior Honeypot? Don't you believe Amber Einstein's dancing around in heaven with your best butt buddy, Jesus?"

I nodded. "It is true that I believe in life after death, a glorious rebirth where we are remade perfectly in God's image, but surely you understand that we still feel the sting of shedding our mortal coil."

"Oh, fuck you."

She rolled her eyes heavenward, disgusted. I considered counseling her further, but she was clearly too simple to understand the concept I was trying to convey and she didn't have a solid enough spiritual footing to take it on faith. So be it. Even though we are all imperfect vessels, we're perfect in the eyes of God, otherwise known as the *Ojo de Dios* if you ask the Huichol Indians of Jalisco, Mexico.

The Bitch Witch glared at me. "I'm warning you, Icefloe. Whatever fancy shit you're thinking right now, you better not fucking *say* it, or I will fling monkey spunk at you and curse you to shit blood for all eternity. I'm serious."

I shrugged. "Fine. Look, if I'm bothering you, you can always get rid of me by sending me to my final instructor."

She nodded. "God, yes. I can't even stand the *sight* of you right now." She took a calming breath. "Okay, so far you've learned how to express yourself spiritually and intellectually. Now, God help us, you must learn how to express yourself *emotionally* so that you can make Pandora cuuuuuum."

"Fine. And who do I see to learn that?"

She leaned in so close that I could see every throbbing vein in her bloodshot green eyes. "There is only one person alive capable of teaching pure emotion to you. *Kathleen, the blind lactation consultant of Cedars-Sinai!*"

Twenty-Four

I ENTERED THE breastfeeding clinic at Cedars-Sinai hospital to find the shock of my life. There were over twenty women there, tits out, chatting happily with each other while babies sucked on their racks like miniature vampires.

"Oh, God," I shouted. "Get those nasty things off your beautiful juggs! They're *ruining* them."

This was a medically accurate diagnosis, by the way. Prolonged breastfeeding can change the shape of a tit, making them less fuckable over time. It was, frankly, kind of sickening to see women's breasts used for a purpose for which they were not intended.

"You must be Jack Icefloe Jackson," a voice said from the back of the room.

I turned to see a woman staring at me. She smiled warmly, although her eyes looked off in all kinds of crazy directions. Even though she was as blind as a bat, that didn't stop her from being a super sexy, completely bangable black chick. By the way, her being black was just fine by me. I've never believed it was fair to deny bitches my cock solely on the basis of skin color. I hope you are as enlightened.

"I am Jack Icefloe Jackson," I said. "I need you to teach me emotion."

"I'll certainly do my best. My name is Kathleen, and it's a pleasure to meet you. Please, come into my office so we can chat." She knocked into chairs and desks as she led me, stumbling, into her office. It was small and warm, like a womb. Big fluffy pillows were everywhere. "Please, have a seat," she said. I did and she sat next to me, taking my hands in hers. They were soft and motherly. "So I understand you're trying to save us all?"

"Yeah."

"And you need to learn how to connect emotionally with women in order to do that?"

"Yeah."

She smiled. "Then you are in luck. The key to connecting emotionally with women is really very simple. You just have to care about their feelings."

I stared at her. "Their what?"

"Their *feelings*. You know, the way they feel about things."

"Wait, whose feelings are we talking about here?"

"Women."

"Okay." I tried to process this. "Hold on. So you're telling me that women ..." I knew she was trying to make a point, but it wouldn't quite come into focus. "You know what? I'm lost."

"Not to worry. Let's just try a little exercise, shall we? Why don't you ask me how my day is going?"

"Why?"

"To demonstrate that you care."

"But I don't."

"Just try."

"I really don't. Seriously."

"Please." She gave me that warm smile again.

I sighed. This was going to be harder than finding a mathematical proof to Fermat's Last Theorem, which, by the way, I fucking solved even though it's unsolvable. "Okay," I said. "How's your day going?"

"Well, I'm glad you asked! It started out well, but do you know what? When I went to brew my coffee this morning I found out that I didn't have any more coffee beans left. So I thought I'd call my friend, Sheila, to see if she had some. Sheila always helps me out. So I picked up my phone and—"

"Jesus fucking Christ, just shoot me now," I interrupted. "Just put a bullet in my fucking brain before I have to listen to any more of this shit." Kathleen stared at me with a shocked expression, which was disconcerting because her blind, broken eyes were looking off in different directions. It was awkward and, for a moment, I felt like maybe I had messed up. "I'm sorry," I said. "You were saying?"

"Yes. Well, I was just telling you that I decided to call my friend Sheila and—"

"*Stop.*" I was on the verge of losing consciousness. "Look, I know it's probably wrong, but I just can't take hearing you blabber like that. If this is what connecting emotionally with women is about, I'm out. The world will just have to die."

Kathleen pursed her lips and then leaned forward, so close that our noses almost touched. She looked very serious, the way a guy will look when he's trying really hard to cum, but then he thinks of his fat buddy's stomach being cut open during a gastric bypass operation and his cock goes limp. "Who hurt you, Icefloe?"

"Huh?"

"Tell Kathleen. You have a deep pain buried away somewhere inside your heart. A terrible wound that hasn't yet healed. You've built emotional walls. I want to help you knock them down."

"Okay. Hey, why are your juggs leaking?"

"What?"

I pointed to her blouse, which was now sopping wet. "Oh, sorry," she said. "That's just mother's milk. I think we're on the verge of a breakthrough, and it got me to lactating. Let's just get back to my question, okay? Who hurt you, Icefloe?"

I shrugged. "I have no idea."

"I think you do. Something happened to you when you were a child. What was it? Open your heart to me. Share with Kathleen."

I tried hard to think of something, but my memories were as empty as a corpse's vagina. "Nope. Nothing. Sorry to disappoint you, but I just had a totally normal childhood."

It was the truth, but Kathleen didn't seem to believe it. She kept after me like a sperm stalking an egg through that Freddy Krueger-like basement of horrors known as the fallopian tubes.

"Tell me about your parents," she said. "What was your mother like?"

"Real nice. Warm. Great big tits. Like you."

"How sweet. Thank you. And your father?"

I shrugged. "I don't know. He was just a regular guy, I guess. Used to take me fishing on the Salmon River, which is where we lived in Alaska. I always thought he had a cool first name: Slade."

Kathleen nodded. "That *is* a nice name. Slade Jackson from Salmon River." Suddenly, her expression sort of changed. "Wait a minute. Do you mean Slade Jackson the *Butcher of Salmon River?*"

"Oh, you've heard of him?"

Her blind eyes went wide. "Of course I've heard of him. He's a famous serial killer! He's on death row in San Quentin. He's killed dozens of people."

"Well, listen to Negative Nancy. He wasn't all bad."

"Wasn't all bad? He was horrible! *He ate your mother!*"

"What are you talking about?" I was having a little trouble understanding her, maybe because her crazy eyes were so disorienting.

"Slade Jackson," Kathleen replied, speaking slowly, "the Butcher of Salmon River, murdered multiple women and ate his wife."

"Ate his wife, right," I echoed. I knew that. Why was she making such a big deal of it?

"His wife," she said, taking my hands in hers. "*Your mother.*"

She seemed to be trying hard to make a point. "And when you say *your mother* …"

"I mean *your mother*. The woman who gave birth to you. The woman whose lactating breasts nursed and nourished you. That woman was eaten by your father."

I puzzled through that for a moment. "So … if I'm understanding you right … what you're saying is that my dad ate my mom?"

"Famously. You must have known this but kept it buried deep within your subconscious because it was too painful to confront." She touched my face with her warm hands. "Do you remember, Jack?"

"I … gosh, I guess I do."

And that's when it hit me—my dad had eaten my mother. For years, I'd kept that bottled up inside me, locked away just like you lock up girlie mags in an airplane carry-on so you don't get tempted to jerk off like a monkey on Ritalin during a transcontinental flight.

"My God," I said. "I haven't thought about that in years. I wonder if that was the turning point in my relationship with him? We've not spoken since."

Kathleen stood. "Jack Icefloe Jackson, I believe we've uncovered why you distance yourself emotionally from women. You don't want to get too close to them, because you don't want to lose them like you lost your mother to your monster of a father."

"Well, I wouldn't exactly call him a—"

"*He's a monster!*"

Was she right? Was my pop really a monster? Was it *possible* that there were things my father did when I was just a boy that led directly to some of the difficulties I now faced with Pandora? The thought staggered me.

"So what should I do?" I asked her.

Once again, she took my hands in hers. She liked doing that. "You must confront your father, Icefloe. We will go together to San Quentin. You will see him, and you will forgive him for his terrible evils, and then you will put him out of your mind forever, moving on from him *so completely* that the emotional healing will begin."

That did not sound like a barrel of fun.

"Fine," I said with a sigh. "Let's just get this shit over with."

Twenty-Five

SAN QUENTIN PENITENTIARY has a regular death row and a super-secret death row for the worst of the worst. My dad was on super-secret death row.

They wouldn't let us into the same room with him for fear he'd eat us, but we were allowed to talk to him through his cell bars. He was chained to the walls just like that hot chick on Skull Island who was tied up by the natives so that King Kong would leave them alone while he finger banged her in that movie whose name I can never remember, just like I can never remember the name of that one about the Wizard of Oz.

"Hi, Dad," I said to him. He was an old, bald guy with muscled arms and a black beard that hung down to his fat belly. He wouldn't even look my way. "It's me, Dad. Icefloe. Your son."

At the mention of son, he spat on the floor. "I have no son. A son *talks* to his father. You haven't talked to me in years."

"Well … you ate Mom."

"*And you'll never let me forget it, will you?* Why did you come here?"

Truth is, I wasn't entirely sure. I knew I was supposed to

forgive him and move on and then emotional healing was going to happen. Or something. I turned to Kathleen for support. She squeezed my hand encouragingly, which gave me the strength I needed to continue.

"Okay, here it is: You're a bad guy and not just because you ate Mom. You did other bad things too. This blind, black lactation consultant here tells me I'm supposed to forgive you, but I just can't. So I guess I came here to tell you that I'm done with you. You claim you have no son. Well, I have no father. There. That's it. Now I can begin to heal emotionally."

Dad began to laugh. It was not the kind of happy, cheerful laugh that sometimes comes out of children. This was the other kind. "Oh, you whiny little douche," he said. "Do you think I *care* what you think? You're an embarrassment. A joke. You're the worst thing that ever happened to me, and to put that in perspective, remember I'm currently on death row scheduled to be executed by firing squad. You take after your dead tasty mother, boy. Spineless and weak."

That filled me with rage. "I am not spineless and I am not weak. In fact, I'm much stronger than you."

"Oh really? How many people have *you* killed?"

I quickly tried to do the calculation in my head. There was the airline ticket counter guy. And that nerdy little poet at Sarah Lawrence University. Plus a few cardinals, although I wasn't sure how many exactly. Seven-ish, maybe? And then there was Mother Superior Honeypot and Amber Einstein, although their deaths weren't technically my fault. I mean, I didn't personally kill them. The universe sort of did that. Plus you had to make a judgment call on my dead wife Tina's passing. Again, I didn't kill her, but she took her own life because she felt she didn't deserve me—and she was totally right about that. Coming up with an accurate total was tough. "I'm gonna say nine," I said finally. "Yup. A total of nine, possibly ten people. So let's just call it eleven. Eleven-ish people."

He rolled his eyes. "That's it? I've killed dozens, you pansy. *Dozens!*"

I stepped closer to the bars. "And look where it's landed you, Pop. Chained like an animal in a cell on death row."

"So what? I *like* it here. But you, if you were chained up next to me you'd be crying like a little schoolgirl. I can just hear you now. *'Boo hoo hoo … stop fucking me in my ass, Dad … boo hoo hoo.'*"

"That's enough. You're embarrassing yourself."

He jumped forward, straining against his chains. "Well, at least I'm not a little liar."

"I'm *not* a little liar."

"Oh, yes, you are. If you'd really wasted eleven people, you'd be here on death row like me. Why aren't you on death row?!"

"Because I have a license to kill, that's why!"

He started laughing that humorless, unfunny laugh again. "Well, la-di-da. Look at the fancy boy with his fancy little license to kill."

"Don't mock me."

"Then don't be so mockable, mocking bird!" He began to tweet like a mocking bird. "*Tweet-tweet!* Daddy's favorite little mocking bird! *Tweet-tweet-tweet!*"

"Stop that."

"Or what—you'll kill me with your super-duper license to kill? See, it's easy to kill someone when they *let* you do it, fairy. A real man kills people the illegal way."

I threw up my hands in disgust. "This is ridiculous. I don't want to get trapped in some kind of pointless, circular argument with you. Let's just agree to disagree."

He shook his head. "No. I *don't* agree to disagree."

"Look, Dad, I'm sorry but you *have* to agree to disagree. Because if you disagree about agreeing to disagree then it's a double negative, which means you *agree*, which is exactly what you *don't* want to do."

He stared at me blankly. "What the fu—"

"I'm just saying that you can't *not* agree to disagree because then you are de facto agreeing. I mean, it's so fucking obvious. Jesus!"

"What the hell are you getting so upset about?" Dad said. "We're just *talking*."

Kathleen rubbed my back. "If you can't find it in your heart to forgive your father for his sins, I think it's best we be going."

Dad turned to her as if noticing her for the first time. "What's with the blind Negress?"

"Oh, *stop it*, Dad."

"What? What did I do *now*? Jesus Christ, I can't say anything around you."

I shook my head. "You just don't get it, do you? You're a sad, lonely man who has eaten the only person who ever loved him. You know what? I pity you."

I turned to go.

"And I pity you, too," he said. "Know why?"

Every synapse in my brain told me not to, but I turned back anyway. "Why?"

"Because no one loves you either, Icefloe. Sure, bitches love your cock, but you got that from me—minus an inch, of course."

"I got six, and six is more than enough. Hell, I don't even use the last inch because it would cause a rip in the fabric of time."

"Keep dreaming, sweet potato." Then he smiled that killer smile of his. "Remember, you're all alone Icefloe. No one in this world loves you. And no one ever will."

That stopped me cold. Was it true? Was I completely unloved? I mean, sure, all chicks wanted me to bang them anally but that was just sex. Was sex actually different from love? Had I confused the two? I felt like Pluto, not the weird dog cartoon, but the thing that used to be a planet that was now just some sad fucking ball of ice spinning out there in the emptiness of space.

Was my dad right?

Was I truly unloved?

"He is *not* unloved," Kathleen said. The strong sound of her voice surprised me. "And to prove it, I am going to *make love* to him. Right here. Right now. Right on this cold hard prison floor."

"Uh, Kathleen," I said. "That's really not necessary. And the floor's sort of dirty, too."

She cupped my face in her hands. "But I'm afraid it is necessary, Icefloe. You have always equated sex with love. But I'm now going to use the power of my 'gina to inject you with real love, *my* love, so that your journey to the world of emotion can be complete."

"Okay, but if you do that, I think it might kill you. In fact, if history is any indication, it definitely will."

She began unbuttoning her blouse. "The very fact that you are concerned about that, concerned for my safety, tells me that you are ready. Take me, Icefloe. Take me hard."

I felt sort of bad about it, but I did as she asked.

It ended up being *awesome*. Under the furious eyes of my father (who kept muttering that his hand was itching for his beloved cleaver), Kathleen and I melded into a seamless unit of white-hot fuckery. Her giant tits flew in the air like toddlers in a bounce house, and her breast milk sprayed the walls like the world's worst dairy accident. She was absolutely amazing. And when she came, all of her emotion shot out of her pussy, down my hard shaft and into my heart, where it filled me with empathy and love.

When it was over, I heard Kathleen shout, "I can see! I can finally see!"

"What do you see?" I asked her. "*Tell me what you see!*"

"The face of God," she said.

"Does he look like Ricardo Montalban?"

She nodded. "Sure does." And then she died, evaporating into mist.

There was silence for a moment until Dad said, "Well, that was fucking unexpected."

I couldn't help it. I began to weep uncontrollably. Weep like I'd never wept before, which isn't really saying much because I had never actually wept before. I turned to my dad, tears streaming down my stubbly cheeks, finally ready to do what I'd come there to do. "I forgive you, Pop," I said. "I forgive you for all your sins, and now I'm moving on from you forever. It is time for me to begin the process of emotionally healing."

"Oh, shut the fuck up, you little pussy. Hey, before you take off, would you mind giving your old man a quick reach around?"

"No, Dad. And you know what? That is *inappropriate.*"

I walked away from him then and headed to the Bitch Witch for a final time.

Twenty-Six

SHE WAS BACK in her hovel on the Upper East Side, throwing cats into a boiling kettle when I arrived. "You again!" she said, yelling above all the frantic meowing.

I nodded.

"Did you find Kathleen the blind lactation consultant of Cedars-Sinai?"

I nodded again.

"And did you fuck her?"

I nodded once more.

"Good," she said. "How was it?"

I tried to answer, but the experience had been so profound that it was hard to talk about it without weeping. In fact, I'd been finding it hard to do anything without weeping. Hell, in the cab on the way from the airport, I saw a billboard advertising a feminine hygiene product that showed a pretty, clean-scrubbed young girl holding a little beagle puppy. It had reduced me to heaving sobs.

The Bitch Witch's eyes narrowed suspiciously. "What's wrong with you? Wait a minute … are you starting to *cry?*"

"No, no, I'm fine." I held up one finger while struggling to get my feelings under control. "Whew. Okay. That's better. It's just … I'm a changed man."

"Why? Because you finally got some emotion in you?"

I shook my head. "No, it's not that. Or at least not *just* that. I have a theory about it, actually, if you want to hear it. I call it my Stool Theory."

"You have a theory about shit?"

"No stool, as in a stool you sit on. You see, this meta-phorical stool of mine has three legs, one for each discipline of the sensitivity quest upon which you sent me: a spiritual leg, an intellectual leg, and an emotional leg. Initially, I learned how to be spiritual and intellectual. But, as wonderful as that was, I had only achieved two legs of my stool, and you can't very well sit on a stool with only two legs, now can you?"

"I guess not," she said, throwing another cat into the kettle.

"Trust me, you can't. In fact, it wasn't until I got the third leg, the *emotional* leg, that my stool finally became useable. Now I can actually sit on my stool of sensitivity! It all just snapped into glorious focus for me, a beautiful rainbow of awareness. Where before I was simply a two-dimensional cartoon, a wooden puppet aimlessly wandering the world like Pinocchio, now I am fully three-dimensional. *I am a real boy!* And finally I feel that I understand the wants and needs and desires of women. They have *emotions*, you know? Just like regular people do! Can you believe it? And the thoughts in their head are complicated and complex. They have feelings—rich, conflicted feelings. They give life and nurture life. They are capable of love, just like men, and they suffer loss, just as we do. They are complete human beings, the real deal, the total package … just as now am I."

I burst into tears.

The Bitch Witch stared at me. "Fag."

"Why must you always be so hurtful?!"

She sighed. "I don't know. I guess I just can't stand to see you like this."

I began to pace. "It's just so much to absorb. I've been reevaluating my previous behavior, and I have to tell you, I'm not completely proud of everything I've done. Some people might even go so far as to call it sexist, misogynistic, homophobic, insensitive … there's probably a few others I'm missing."

"You could probably toss racist in there."

"My point is: The person who acted like that is gone. I'm different now. I'm going to dedicate my life to becoming a shining beacon of male sensitivity. I'm *changed*, Bitch Witch."

The Bitch Witch nodded. "Yeah, I can see that. And you know what? I finally think you're ready."

"For …?"

"Pandora. Seeing you like this absolutely disgusts me. Right now, as far as I'm concerned, you are the least appealing man on the planet. And seeing as how Pandora is my exact opposite, it means you're finally ready to fuck her and make her cuuuuuum. She likes whiny pussies like you."

"Thank you, Bitch Witch," I said, tears welling up in my eyes. "Thank you for all you've done."

"Oh, Jesus, just get the hell out of here already. You're making me sick." She threw another cat into the kettle.

I took a few calming breaths to bring myself under control and then headed out to find Pandora.

Twenty-Seven

PANDORA WAS SITTING on a grassy bluff under a glorious oak tree back at the campus of Sarah Lawrence University, surrounded by her friends from the Victoria's Secret catalogue. I was aware that she might have some negative feelings toward me because of my behavior the last time I courted her, so I knew I had a rather deep hole from which to dig myself. I walked up to her, mesmerized by her almost supernatural beauty.

"Excuse me, Pandora?"

She glanced up. "Yes?" And then her face filled with disgust. "Oh, God. You again? I have nothing to say to you. You're repulsive. Please leave." How I loved her sexy British accent! So smart and United Kingdom-ish.

I nodded. "I understand your feelings. And I just want you to know that I am truly ashamed of my behavior the last time I came to seek your affections. My only defense is that I was a different man at the time, a base and formless creature. I have since gone on a quest of sensitivity and enlightenment, and I wish to apologize. Truly."

She stared at me, still somewhat unsure. "Okay."

From behind my back, I withdrew a bouquet of yellow daisies, freshly plucked from the rich loam of the earth. "For you."

"They're ... they're beautiful."

"Next to you, they pale in comparison."

She took them and then stood up on her long, coltish legs. They were strong and young. "Let me ask you a question," she said. "Why yellow daisies? Why not roses? Aren't they more traditional?"

I shook my head. "Roses signify love, my lady, and I have not yet earned your love. It would be presumptuous of me to prematurely give something so rich in meaning to such a lovely bitch as you."

"A what?"

"I mean, such a lovely *woman* as you. Sorry. Old habits ..." I chuckled.

She nodded. "It's okay." Then she sniffed the daisies. "Oooh, they're just wonderful. Thank you."

"No thank *you*, just for being you." My pulse raced as I contemplated posing my next question. "Pandora?"

"Yes?"

"Might I ... might I call on you again? I understand there's a delicious yogurt shop in town. I'm told you can choose your own toppings, up to three."

She considered for a moment and then smiled. "That would be nice. I'd like that." The Victoria's Secret models around her clapped happily.

And so began the best few days of my life.

Pandora and I became inseparable, giggling together like schoolgirls. We ran hand in hand through the flowering meadows, the air clean and fresh and kissed by the first whisper of spring. We painted each other's toenails. She chose plum. I chose fire engine red. The hours were a marvelous blur of picnics and shared secrets and rosy dreams of the future, here and in the afterlife. We both believed in a life after this one, of course, where we would join with all the souls that have ever lived and be made perfect in the eyes of God.

"You know, the Huichol Indians of Jalisco, Mexico, have a phrase for that," she said.

I smiled and stroked her cheek. "Yes, my darling. *Ojo de Dios*."

"You *do* know!"

We diagrammed sentences together and solved famous unsolved mathematical problems, the Birch and Swinnerton-Dyer conjecture among them. As you know, I had already conquered Fermat's Last Theorem. We read the *Iliad* to each other and plumbed the hidden depths of James Joyce's *Ulysses*. We even talked about getting married. We'd get a dog together, we decided. She was fond of golden retrievers, but I was newly partial to labradoodles.

"Let's get both!" she exclaimed, and we delightedly clapped our hands as if trying to bring Tinker Bell back to life.

She wanted children, and so did I. We decided to have two. She wanted a boy so that he would one day grow up to be, as she said, "Just like you, Jack." I, of course, wanted Daddy's little girl, a beautiful dress up doll to put in frilly pink outfits. A tea party companion with whom to eat cucumber sandwiches while sipping from delicate china cups, pinkies raised.

Oh, how we laughed!

But even though we were living in a perfect bubble of happiness, all the while a dark cloud hung over us. Pandora's twenty-first birthday was drawing near, and we were keenly aware that if we didn't have premarital sex soon, and if she didn't climax, the Earth was doomed. But I didn't want to pressure her. It was either to happen because she desired it or not at all, world be damned. Pardon my French.

Finally, on the night before her twenty-first birthday, with only six hours to spare, she turned to me and said, "I'm ready, Jack."

"Are you sure?" I asked. "I don't want to rush anything."

She cupped my face in her soft hands. "Never worry about that. You've been wonderful. I truly want to do this with you. Make love to me, Jack. Lay me down on this picnic blanket here under the stars and fill me and make me whole."

"As you wish," I said as I gently lay her down.

That's when we were shot by tranquilizer darts. "Oww!" Pandora yelled. "Jack, what's happening?"

"I got hit, too," I said, clutching her, my consciousness fading fast. I looked up to see a gorgeous woman in a skintight black dominatrix outfit with a swastika on the armband. She held a riding crop.

"Who … who are you?" I asked.

"I am Ilsa," she said, "Nazi Bitch of the SS, and you are now my prisoners. I am taking you to *Fuhrer Island*!"

Twenty-Eight

I AWOKE TO Find myself strapped to a stainless steel table, completely naked, deep in the underground lair of the Nazi Bitches of the SS. "Pandora?" I called out, looking around.

"Here, Jack," she replied. They had stripped her naked and locked her in a metal cage that hung from the ceiling. It broke my heart to see her like that. "Are you okay?" she asked.

I nodded. "I'm fine. I just want you to know that, whatever happens, I love you."

"And I, you, Jack."

"How sweet," a voice said, dripping with sarcasm the same way a penis will drip with semen for a few minutes after climax. I looked over to see Ilsa standing there in her dominatrix outfit, smacking her riding crop on the palm of an outstretched hand. She was flanked on either side by ten more identical Nazi Bitches, all with the same short cropped blonde hair and cruel blue eyes. "Welcome …" Ilsa said, "to Fuhrer Island!"

They all did the Nazi salute and shouted: "*Seig heil!*"

"Who are you?" I asked. "I know you said your name was Ilsa, but I thought she died years ago."

"We are her clones, duplicated from cells harvested from the left nipple of the original."

Well, that figured. Evil never dies, does it? "What do you want with us?"

Ilsa number one walked toward me then with a sadistic grin on her face. "Not much, really. We just want to prevent you from making *das sex*!"

"*Nein! Nein on das sex*!" the clones of Ilsa shouted.

"But if Pandora and I don't make love and if she doesn't climax, the Earth is doomed. In fact," I looked around, "what time is it?"

"One hour until midnight," Ilsa number one replied. "Which is one hour until Pandora's twenty-first birthday, which is when the world will end in the name of *das Fuhrer*!"

Another "*Sieg heil!*" from those evil bitches.

So that was their plan. They wanted to prevent Pandora and I from making sweet, sweet love, which meant Pandora would never orgasm, which meant the apocalypse was at hand. And all in the name of their precious dead Fuhrer.

"Jack," Pandora said. "Something's wrong. I hear ticking."

I listened intently. Sure enough, I heard it too. "Wait. Is that your—"

"Yes," she said with a nod. "My vagina is ticking. Soon it's going to explode and form a black hole. We don't have much time."

I turned to Ilsa number one. "Please, you must let us have intercourse. You *must*."

"*Nein!*" she shouted. "But don't worry, Jack Icefloe Jackson. Even though you won't be fucking Pandora, your fine dick will not go unused this evening because *we* are going to fuck you. In fact, we are going to fuck you *to death*!"

All the Nazi Bitches laughed cruelly, which is the only way Nazi Bitches know how to laugh.

"I will begin with *das fuckery*," Ilsa number one said, stripping off her shiny leather outfit to reveal an evilly perfect body created by the devil himself to lure men and bi-curious women to the hot molten gates of hell.

"No," I said. "Please, I can't make love to you. You must understand. I am saving myself for my soulmate—"

"Too late," the first clone of Ilsa snapped as she lowered herself onto my stiff member. I could feel her sliding down. First one inch … then two. She began moaning in pleasure.

"Slow down," I said. "You're moving too fast. You're already at the second inch. You don't want to go much further. Danger lies ahead."

"More," she groaned in ecstasy. "Must have *more*. Must have Jack Icefloe Jackson's third inch." She slid down to the third inch. And then to the fourth. Her hot Nazi body was vibrating like an idling Harley. "Yes … yes!"

"No," I said. "You must stop before it's too late. You won't survive the fifth inch, and I've caused too much death already."

"MORE!" she yelled, lowering herself onto the fifth inch, the very same one that had destroyed the Fuck-Bot. "Oh, God! So good!" She was shaking now like a bucket in a paint mixer. "Delicious! Delicious! Must have more!"

"No!" I shouted. "You can't take the sixth inch—no one can! It will cause a rip in the fabric of time!"

"I want it! *Gimme, gimme, gimme!*" Against my will, she slipped down onto the sixth inch, and her eyes snapped open like roller blinds. "Yes! Yes! *YES!*"

The smell of sulfur began to emanate from her and the air became electric. Lightning cracked throughout the Nazi lair, and suddenly, a gaping hole in the very fabric of time ripped open behind her, a swirling purple gash in the wall of eternity. She saw it and, eyes wide with panic, tried to run but it was too late. It sucked her, screaming, into the black abyss and then slammed shut with a thunderous *crack!* The lightning stopped, the electricity in the air dissipated and soon all was quiet and still.

Ilsa number one was gone.

"I told her to beware the sixth inch," I said to the other Nazi bitches, gasping and sweating. "I *warned* her."

Ilsa number two stepped forward and began to strip off her outfit. "My turn. I want that meaty sixth inch all to myself."

I was in shock. Was this really happening? "But … but it just killed Ilsa number one."

Ilsa number two spat in disgust. "Feh. She was always weak. I am strong. I am better than her. I am Ilsa number *two*. I can take all *das cock*!"

"But you're her identical clone. If she couldn't take it, neither can you. My God, no one can. You must stop!"

"*Nein!*" she yelled and then lowered herself onto my majestic scepter.

Do I even have to tell you what happened? Moaning in evil ecstasy, she worked her way down to the apocalyptic sixth inch. And then there was that sulfur smell again, followed by the crack of lightning as electricity filled the air, growing and growing in intensity until *another* gaping purple hole ripped through the fabric of time, leading into a realm of nightmare. It sucked her in and then slammed closed.

"Unbelievable," I said, staring in shock.

Ilsa number three approached me then. "Now *my turn*."

"Seriously? You're kidding me!"

She laughed hollowly. "Ilsa number one and number two were like *das children*. I am Ilsa number *three*. I am woman! I can take all Jack Icefloe Jackson's meatrod!" Eyes wild with rapture, she straddled me and went to work.

By the way, just in case you're having trouble picturing exactly how my cock functioned in this situation, I've taken the liberty of drawing an illustration for you, detailing it inch by inch:

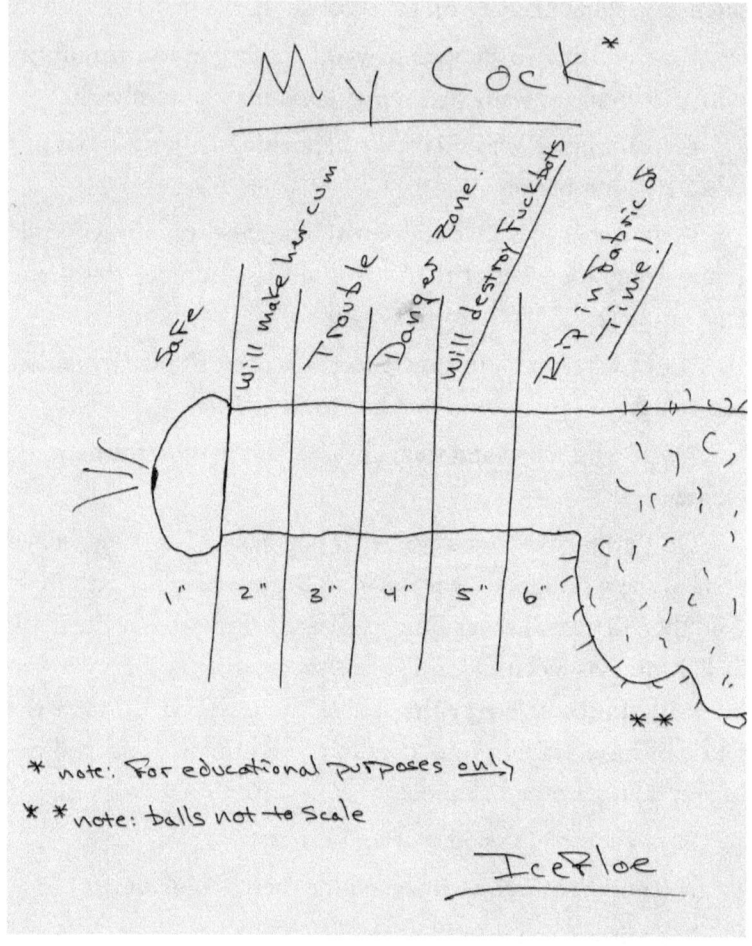

Even though I was in agony from the abuse of the clones, it was not without benefit. While each Nazi Bitch rode me, destroying themselves on my sixth inch like Army Rangers running into machine gun nests on Omaha Beach, something incredible happened. As I lay there, imagining myself far away in a tropical paradise with my beloved, I realized that my Stool

Theory from before had been all wrong. As any good carpenter will tell you, the best stools do not have three legs but *four*. In my journey of self-discovery, I had forgotten all about the most important leg of all.

My cock.

As each of my captors was sucked screaming into the abyss, I melded my sexuality with my newfound spirituality, intellect and emotion. I became strong—a man-ingot, forged in a crucible of torment. By hardening my resolve along with my pecker, those evil women had actually done me, and the world, a favor.

I was finally ready.

Soon every Nazi Bitch was dead, and Pandora and I found ourselves alone, stranded on Fuhrer Island.

"Are you okay, Jack?" she asked.

Gasping, weak, I answered. "Yes, my love."

"Good," she said. Her vagina was ticking feverishly. "I'm afraid we don't have much time."

"Then let's do this."

My sweat had greased the bonds that held me, and I was able to slip out of them and free myself. I climbed up to the cage that contained Pandora, unlocked it and freed her. We were now just two naked, brutalized people whose love had to be strong enough to save the world.

"Enter me, Jack. Fill me with your essence. I'm ready."

"So am I, baby."

I entered her holy of holies, her pagan temple, her Egyptian tomb. It was like sliding into a hot buttered muffin baked by God himself. I brought a lifetime of cocking skill to bear, along with all the sensitivity that had been gifted to me by the three marvelous women who gave their lives to save all of ours.

"Yes, Jack," Pandora moaned. "Just like that. Deeper."

I was already up to the third inch. I slipped her the fourth.

"Oh, yes …" she gasped.

My mind raced back to the happy days we'd shared together while falling in love. The laughter, the tears. The dreams of a new life together. Marriage. *A family*.

"The fifth inch, Jack!" she screamed. "I need it!"

"No," I said, shaking my head. "You've got too much in you already. You won't be able to take it."

"Give it to me! I have to have it!"

Nervously, I slipped her the fifth inch. Instantly, her body responded. She vibrated like a tuning fork, alive with sexual energy. "Yes, Jack," she said. "I feel you! I'm close!"

"Then cum for me, baby. Cum for the *world*!"

The ticking of her pussy was faster now, a blinding shriek of sound. We had only seconds left before detonation.

"You almost there?" I asked. "God knows I am."

"I need more!" she screamed. "Just a little more to put me over the top! *I need the sixth inch!*"

"No! Never, my love! I will not give it to you! It will destroy you!"

"*I have to have it!*"

"Please, baby, don't make me do this!"

She grabbed my face and, looking deep into my eyes, said, "Do it, Jack. Do it now. Do it for *us*. I love you so much."

"And I, you," I said and then slipped her my sixth and final inch.

Twenty-Nine

THE EARTH TREMBLED as Pandora and I were seamlessly joined. Like an installation of hardwood floors, I was the tongue and she was the groove, and we tongued and grooved our way to sweet oblivion.

"YES, JACK!" she screamed as a sulfur smell filled the air.

"Hold on!" I yelled. "It's happening again! Another rip in the fabric of time! And it's gonna be a big one!"

Lightning cracked, thunder crashed and the hugest gaping purple gash that the world had ever seen ripped across the face of reality right behind her, opening into the abyss. It sucked at us like a category 5 tornado, a perfect storm pulling us toward it with a cold, godless embrace.

"Are you almost there?" I shouted.

"Almost, Jack! Just a few seconds more!" She bounced up and down on my mighty staff like an energetic toddler on grandpa's knee. "*Yes, yes, yes!*"

"*I'm cumming, too!*" I shouted as a white hot spike of ecstasy shot through me. The rip in the fabric of time raged violently behind us while a hurricane of memory and emotion tore across the landscape of my mind—intimate secrets shared with my beloved, our first date over yogurt with three free toppings, the promise of a wide green lawn filled with golden retriever puppies and leaping labradoodles, tea parties with my daughter-to-be complete with china cups and raised pinkies.

In that moment, everything coalesced into a perfect stew of love and bliss and ecstasy. And, just then, like a chorus of angels whispering to me from the afterlife, I heard my beloved dead wife, Tina, along with Mother Superior Honeypot, Amber Einstein and Kathleen the blind lactation consultant of Cedars-Sinai say, "*Shoot that load, big daddy. Shoot that load!*"

I came. Hard.

So did Pandora.

My spunk shot out of me and into her in a glorious tsunami of cum, and it contained all the spirituality, intellect and emotion that I had worked so hard and sacrificed so much to acquire over the past week. Complex math equations and empathy for the homeless and deep religious conviction left my body like a bar patron after closing time. And, as it all drained away from me, never to return, my last enlightened thought was, "*My God, this is just like* Flowers for Algernon *but with pussy.*"

And then I had no idea what that meant.

The shrieks of the damned echoed from the abyss as the rip in the fabric of time healed itself and then closed shut. The electricity went out of the air, the sulfur smell dissipated and Pandora collapsed on top of me, spent and exhausted. The ticking sound coming from her vagina had finally stopped.

She sighed happily and then wrapped her arms around me. "You did it, Jack. It's over. You gave me my first orgasm and disarmed my vagina. The world is now safe."

I grunted.

She leaned up on my chest and smiled. "So, what do you think? You think we have a future together? You think I might become *Mrs.* Pandora Icefloe Jackson some day?" She drew circles in the sweaty hair on my fat belly. "Do you think you've finally found your *soulmate*, Jack?"

I thought about it.

"Nah."

Thirty

I NEVER SAW Pandora again. That's the way you have to treat bitches, by the way. Bang 'em and leave 'em wanting more.

Obama was happy. As I stood on the back lawn of the White House, he held up a shiny medal. Ms. Cherry (the woman who'd controlled the Fuck-Bot) was in attendance along with the Bitch Witch, who was smiling, which was disturbing.

"For service above and beyond the call of duty in your quest to save our world," Obama said, "I present *you*, Jack Icefloe Jackson, with America's highest honor: the Medal of Freedom." He went to pin it on my jacket.

"Watch the dynamite," I said.

"Oh. Sorry." He pinned it a little lower. "There we go. So what do you think?"

"Not bad," I said. "Although it's kind of a faggy little medal. You got anything bigger you can give me? Something unique, like the 'Medal of Cock' or something?"

"And he's back!" the Bitch Witch shouted. "The godless, ignorant hick is back!"

"I'm sorry, we don't offer a Medal of Cock," Obama said. "But America, and the world, owes you its deepest debt of gratitude."

I shrugged. "It was no big deal. Making bitches cum is what I do."

"Don't underestimate the seriousness of your accomplishment. Without you, we'd all be dead now."

"That's true," I agreed. "So, I'm guessing you want your license to kill back?"

"Why don't you hang on to it," Obama replied.

"You sure? If I have it, I'll use it. Trust me, there's a lot of people out there that aggravate me, and I've got a shit-ton of dynamite. I have road rage issues."

"Well, I was thinking more that you'd use it in the line of duty. You see, there's another *situation* that has come up that could benefit from your unique abilities."

Uh-oh, I thought. Here we go again …

"What is it?"

"Have you ever heard of a vampiress by the name of Hypatia?"

I shook my head. "Nope."

"She's the ruler of the vampire kingdom, as vicious as she is beautiful. She is feared even by other vampires. She is known as the Suckubus."

"The Suckubus, huh?"

"Vampires, as you know, control the banking industry."

"I didn't know that."

"Well, they do. They suck money out of our economy just like they suck blood out of our veins. Hypatia is as well protected as she is well-funded."

I shifted from one leg to the other. Obama was starting to bore me. "Okay, so what's the problem here? Can we just get skip to the point?"

"Well, the problem is that the Devil is *this close* to choosing Hypatia as his bride. If he does and if they consummate their unholy union, she will bear a vampire devil-child that will give rise to a legion of unstoppable vampire devil-children. If that happens, there is nothing that can be done to save us. They will devour us all."

"So what do you want me to do about it?"

"The Devil will only choose as his bride a *virgin*. So far, Hypatia has been untouched by man. Many have tried, of course, but she has consumed them."

"How?"

"It is rumored that her vagina is ringed with fangs, like the ones in her mouth—it shreds any penis that comes near it."

I let out a long, low whistle. "Ouch."

Obama nodded. "Quite the challenge. Here's what we need from you, Icefloe: You must infiltrate the vampire banking establishment, find Hypatia and deflower her before the Devil does."

"I see. So it's me against the devil, dynamiting bankers and banging hot vamp bitches?"

"If you accept the challenge."

This fucking guy ...

"Are you shitting me?" I said. "Jack Icefloe Jackson has never turned his back on his country before, and I'm sure as hell not about to start now. Let's get this thing done."

"That's the spirit!" Obama said, clapping me on the back.

Cock out, dynamite in hand, I headed off to save the world one more damn time ...

THE END

If you enjoyed this romantic adventure,
please be sure to check out Jack Icefloe
Jackson's next masterpiece:

JACK ICEFLOE JACKSON'S

ROMANCE for

MEN

SUCKUBUS

About the Author

Jack Icefloe Jackson lives in the Alaskan wilderness. His hobbies include dynamite fishing and fucking Chinese bitches because they so horny.

www.ingramcontent.com/pod-product-compliance
Lightning Source LLC
Chambersburg PA
CBHW021106130626
46554CB00002B/563